Burdens

Stories by Drew Kizer

BURDENS

6909 Timber Trail Road
Leeds, AL 35094
drewkizer.com

Published by Riddle Creek Publishing
252 Cypress Creek Drive
Florence, AL 35633
riddlecreekpublishing.com

Cover artwork and illustrations by Jacob Hennigan
Jacket layout by Allison Kizer

ISBN: 978-0-9835009-6-4

To Mom, who kept good books on our shelves.

Contents

bur·den

/ˈbərdn/ *noun* 1: a: something that is carried: LOAD; b: DUTY, RESPONSIBILITY; 2: something oppressive or worrisome; 3: a: a central topic: THEME; b: CHORUS, REFRAIN; 4: *ARCHAIC:* **something uttered, esp. by God or a prophet.**

Malevolent, pupilless eyes gazed back at the old man as he examined the piece.

A People at Sea

A bell chimed as the door of the little shop opened, alerting the shopkeeper to the entrance of an old man wearing a shabby hide. The old man dropped into one of the chairs the shopkeeper had on display, took a filthy-looking rag from his leather bag, and mopped his bald head, shining it as if it were a precious gem. The shopkeeper cast a flimsy smile in the old man's direction and returned to the conversation he had been having with his friend, who flared out his nostrils and lowered his eyebrows at the odor that had trailed the old man into the shop.

"I told her if she expected to continue being my wife, some things had to change," the shopkeeper said, raising his voice toward the end of his declaration to give his friend the impression he was a man accustomed to getting his way. "One broken figure I can let go," he said, "but this makes six in three years of marriage. I won't put up with it. If she can't learn to respect my property, she'll have to go."

His friend stood squarely, facing him with his legs shoulder-width apart, pulling his beard and watching the man with wide, sympathetic eyes.

"Those figures are heirlooms, a set of ten. They can't be replaced, you know."

His friend nodded mutely.

"My parents purchased them from Egyptian merchants in Tekoa. 'Hold onto these, son,' my mother said. 'One day they will be worth a lot of money.' Then this wife of mine carelessly breaks them! I won't put up with it. I told her so."

"Are you talking about toys?" a voice asked from the corner. The two men had already forgotten about the old man, their noses having adjusted to his musk.

"What did you say?" the shopkeeper asked.

"I was asking if you were upset about your toys. It sounds like you're thinking about divorcing your wife because she broke your toys."

"They're not *toys*," the shopkeeper said, offended. "They're part of a set. Heirlooms purchased by my parents when I was little."

"Did you play with them?"

The shopkeeper spun around to look at the old man. "What has that got to do with it? I was a little boy when they gave them to me. I suppose I played with them."

He turned back to his friend, who frowned at the old man as if he were an impudent child and tried to steer the conversation back to the subject of his heroic taste for rare things. "I was always careful, knowing they were very valuable pieces. Even then I had a nose for items of value."

His friend nodded firmly in agreement.

"I was just asking," explained the old man, "because little boys play with toys. If you played with them when you were little, they were toys."

"Sir, they are not *toys*! Now, would you be so kind—"

"Why would you put away your wife for some toys?"

"I can't see how that is any of your business!" shouted the shopkeeper.

"If it were none of my business, you wouldn't be carrying on about it in this here shop."

"Sir, is there something I can do for you, or did you just come in to eavesdrop?" Vagrants were coming into the shop all the time looking for a cool place away from the sun or a cup of water. The shopkeeper accommodated them when he could, but this old man had almost stretched his patience to its limit. He gave up telling his story for the moment and turned to his intruder, intending to throw him out. What an annoyance! How many did this make this week? The shopkeeper had lost count.

"Did you ever think that maybe she's not breaking those toys by accident?" asked the old man. "I mean, six toys in three years! No woman's that careless. I'll bet she's trying to tell you something. Maybe she's *hoping* you'll put her away." The old man chuckled while polishing his head with the rag.

The shopkeeper's powers of speech failed him. Somehow, the old man had reached into his head and pulled the lever that controlled his tongue, a feat no one besides his wife had ever accomplished.

His friend stepped in when he saw that the shopkeeper had been struck dumb by the old man's ribbing. "Mister," he said to the old man, "state your business, or go. We ain't got time for tramps with nothing else to do but barge into establishments and harass honest proprietors like my friend here. Now, you've taken your rest. You best be going before I turn you out."

"My apologies," said the old man, pushing on his staff to rise from his chair. "I did not mean to leave the impression that I was loitering. I was hoping to procure a special item from you. I have not been able to find one in all the shops I have visited so far."

The challenge loosened the shopkeeper's tongue. He moved behind the counter and said, "Maybe you can tell us what you're looking for, and we might be able to help you." These were the moments he lived for. The shop was sacred to him, a temple for lost treasures. He knew every square inch of every shelf and cranny. He had no need for accounting or inventory logs. If someone wanted a stuffed boar's head from Cush or a Nabatean gold coin, and he had it, he knew exactly where it was stored. Above his head hung several knives, daggers, and implements of war. A stack of tattered books rested on the counter near his hands, and to his right a beautiful ibex hide was stretched out on a frame.

The shop was filled with tools, collectibles, garments, books, figurines, bas reliefs, and many other curiosities. They were his closest friends. Old things, unlike people, never denied his wishes, disrespected him, or betrayed him. He could always count on them.

"An item of Babylonian origin," said the old man as he scanned a shelf stacked with old farming equipment. "A clay likeness."

"Could you be more specific?" asked the shopkeeper, now curious.

"I'll know it when I see it."

"Just a minute." The shopkeeper ducked through a curtain that hung behind his counter and entered his storeroom. No one ventured back there but the proprietor himself. That was where he kept the special items, those collectibles that could not be trusted to sit on the shelves.

He returned to the front of the shop after a few minutes, hands full, and found his friend interrogating the old man. "Where you from, old timer?" he asked.

"Israel."

"I know that, you old fool, I mean what part of Israel?"

"I have come out of the wilderness of the Negeb, but I belong to all parts. I'm here just until I find a certain item, one that has a special purpose in this very village."

"I see," said the friend. He glanced over at the shopkeeper and then grinned at the old man's ridiculous garb. "What are you, some kind of a religious fanatic?"

"You could say that, I suppose."

"So what, you like to go around telling people what to do?"

"No, it's not that way. I rarely do what I *like*."

"Nobody's forcing you."

The old man sat down and looked up at the two men in the shop. "I'll tell you a story. One evening I sat beside a fire, warming myself and preparing to turn in for the night. I kept staring at the flames—how they were dancing on the logs of the fire, hopping up and down, just as they have made men do when they try to walk across hot coals. I stared into the orange heat, thinking about how no one really can bear to touch the earth. We're all hopping from one foot to the other, doing some strange dance of survival.

"While I was caught up in this reverie, I saw a vision of God. I dare not describe it to you. I don't think I could if I tried. It doesn't matter what I saw. It's what I *heard* that changed my life: *I have put my words in your mouth*, the voice said, *to break loamless hearts and plow fertile fields. I am sending you out into the cold and the warmth of a people at sea.* When I rose from my fire at dawn, I was heavier than the day before. I have carried that burden with me until now."

"You poor thing," said the shopkeeper's friend, mocking him.

"Well, yes," said the shopkeeper, "I have a few things here that might interest you." He spread two earthen vessels, a large bowl, and a few small pieces of jewelry proudly on the counter before the old man and smiled.

The old man took one look at them and shook his head. "This is not what I'm looking for."

Disappointed, the shopkeeper asked, "What is it exactly that you are looking for?"

"Don't you have anything more—eccentric, if you know what I mean?" The old man winked when he said this.

The shopkeeper smiled broadly. "Yes," he said, "just a minute!" He disappeared behind the curtain again.

He returned with a strange clay mask. The mask depicted a hideous, grinning face. The smile was crammed with teeth on the top and bottom rows and stretched to its limits, so much so that wrinkles covered every part of the mask: its chin, the corners of the mouth, the forehead, and even across the flat, irregular nose. Malevolent, pupilless eyes gazed back at the old man as he examined the piece.

"It's Humbaba, guardian of the cedars of Lebanon," said the shopkeeper, almost in a whisper. "It's very old and very valuable. The Babylonians hang him over their doorways as a charm against evil. Frankly, you surprise me. You didn't strike me as a man who would appreciate a piece like this. You know what I mean. A piece like this, it's, shall we say, *exotic*."

"It's perfect. How much?" asked the old man.

"A piece like this is very valuable. I couldn't easily part with it."

"I have means. Name your price, shopkeeper."

"200?"

"Fine." The old man pulled a little purse from somewhere in the recesses of the dusty hide he wore and counted out the sum as the shopkeeper watched in astonishment. He thanked him, nodded to his wary friend, and headed into the blazing light of the noonday public square.

The square was filled with people of all sorts—mothers with their children examining fruit in the markets, merchants weighing their wares on scales, sailors on shore leave, priests on their way to perform their duties, farmers trailed by their livestock and its refuse, and beggars interrupting the pulse of activity with their pleading. The hot dust rose with every footfall. Above the din of the crowd and the cattle, a hammer was striking iron in the distance.

The old man made for a post standing in the square in front of a tavern. A sign affixed to it read, GRUB HERE. The old man removed the leather belt that cinched his hairy garment together, exposing an interior of hair and ribs and loincloth, and fixed the clay mask to the post using the belt. By now, several eyes were watching him from the crowded mass. They were the only stationary objects in the pulsating heap, like pelicans sitting on the waves of the sea. The old man felt the eyes on him as he worked, although he didn't let on that he noticed.

After he secured the mask to the post, he brought the crowd to attention, shouting, "Welcome to the gallery of fools! Come! Don't be shy! We are going to make some changes to my friend here. Doesn't he look a little unhappy? Perhaps he is constipated, or maybe he had some bad fish. Maybe his wife kicked him out and he had to spend the night in the street!"

Some children gathered at his feet and sat cross-legged on the ground. Some of the women giggled nervously, but the men glowered at the exhibition and stayed in the flow of the crowd.

"Now!" said the man, producing a lump of charcoal, "let's see what we can do about that smile, shall we?" Using the charcoal, he blacked out some of the teeth in the mask's crowded smile. "That's better!" The old man stepped back so that the children could see his work. The smile now looked absurd, like a house with random broken windows.

"Where are his eyebrows?" he asked the children. "The eyebrows reveal emotions. We can't tell if this is a happy little demon…" The old man raised his eyebrows and smiled widely as he said this. "…or a sad little demon…" His countenance fell. "…or an *angry* demon!" He growled as he said this last part, lunging at the children and furrowing his brow while baring his teeth. The children squealed with excitement while their mothers smiled, happy for the distraction. "I think he is a happy little demon!" said the man, and he drew two symmetrical eyebrows on the forehead of the mask, angling them upward to show delight.

"Now, what are we going to do about that hair?" At the top, the clay face featured the border of a straight hairline in the style of the people who sculpted it. "Let's add a little color!" The old man coughed and spat a tremendous wad of saliva and phlegm on the ground and worked it into the dust, making a red dye for the mask's hair. With his fingers, he painted the mask. When he finished, he stepped back to admire his work. The once menacing face now looked stupid and benign. Bright red hair topped the face of a fool, who smiled gaily at the growing crowd through a mouth with gaping holes.

Several men had joined their wives now to watch the spectacle. The children wanted more. "He still needs more color, I think. Don't you?" The children squealed their affirmations. "Who has some fruit?" A little girl handed him a date. "No, I'm afraid that's too hard, my little friend. We wouldn't want to hurt him. Does anyone have some fruit that has spoiled? Something squishy." Another child brought figs. The old man rubbed them into a paste to use on the clay face. He worked the reddish stain into its cheeks, making it blush with embarrassment.

"That looks better, I think! What about you?" The children cheered, but the adults looked uncomfortable.

The old man paused. A disturbance was parting the crowd like a ship's rudder through water. The old man saw an enormous Phoenician burst through, moving people aside with his strong arms like they were flimsy branches in a forest. "That's Humbaba, guardian of the cedars of Lebanon!" he cried. He appeared to be offended by the old man's sideshow. "What have you done? You have vandalized a sacred charm!"

"Oh, he doesn't look too scary to me," said the old man. "I just think he's got a bit of indigestion. Perhaps he had too many raisin cakes last night. He probably has a hard time chewing his food with all those missing teeth." The old man wheezed with an uncontrollable laugh. Tears streamed from his eyes, and he doubled over as he shook with amusement. "Oh yes," he said between outbursts, "he must have had too much fun last night!" This began a fresh round of laughter. The children were laughing. The women tried to hide their smiles.

"Take it down!" said the big Phoenician.

"Now why would I do that?" asked the old man. "We are having so much fun, aren't we children?" The children nodded in agreement. "Maybe you're jealous. Would you like a makeover, too?"

"The head of Humbaba graced the door of Enlil, king of the gods. My mother hung a clay mask just like that one over the door of our home to keep away the evil spirits. It is a sacred charm, and you have insulted it. Take it down. This is your last chance!"

"Who did you say? Lil' En? Never heard of him."

The Phoenician charged toward the mask strapped to the post, but the old man stepped in his way. "I will thank you not to touch my property," he said. With a beastly growl, the Phoenician backhanded him across the cheek. The old man heard every bone in his neck crack. The force of the slap spun him on his heels, but he did not fall. With his foot the Phoenician gave the old man's backside a shove, and he fell face first into the dust at the feet of the children whose faces no longer wore expressions of delight. While the Phoenician fiddled with the mask, trying to remove it from the post, the old man slowly picked himself up and dusted off his hairy cloak, still hanging open because his belt was holding the mask to the post.

"That's my property, I said. Please take your hands off of it." The Phoenician acted as if he didn't hear him. "Can someone help me? This man seems to think this mask belongs to him." The old man looked around at the waiting crowd, but no one moved.

"Well then." The old man walked toward the post where the Phoenician was having trouble undoing the belt and took him by the elbow, his head just barely coming level with the big man's shoulder.

"Get your hands off me!" shouted the Phoenician. He grabbed the old man's cloak by the collar and slung him to the ground hard. Putting his foot on the back of the old man's head, he ground his face into the dust. Pain squeezed through his eyes in tears, and he gritted his teeth in an effort to stay conscious. Still holding the cloak, the Phoenician pulled it up by the collar while keeping the old man on the ground with his foot. The old man felt his shoulders tearing as they were pulled back in their sockets. Finally, the cloak came off. The old man lay in the dust of the square like a plucked chicken.

The children ran away. Most of the crowd receded like a tide timed to respond to violence rather than the suggestions of the moon. It would return the next time some old man was being abused or a wife was being berated in public or some beggar was kicked like trash in the gutter. It was a crowd with an ebb and flow tuned to human misery.

The hot sun baked the old man in the square, and the sand flies slaked their thirst on his tears. He lay alone, like some molting reptile without his skin, while the Phoenician worked on the mask until he finally freed it from the post and walked away examining it in his hand, grumbling to himself as he left.

The shopkeeper stood in his front door, examining the old man from a distance for signs of life. He had heard the commotion from inside his shop and, like the others, dropped what he was doing to watch the spectacle. Now that the show was over, everyone had returned to their business. Was he alive? The shopkeeper couldn't tell.

He grabbed a skin of water and ran into the hot, empty square. The old man must have been able to feel the air cool from his shadow because he rolled over and squinted at the figure hovering over him.

"Hello shopkeeper," he rasped.

"Are you all right?"

"Yes, my son," the old man said as he tried to get up. "I think I'll live."

"Let me help you." The shopkeeper helped him sit up. He took the skin of cool water and gave him a drink and wiped his face with a clean rag. The swollen, purple cheek reminded him of the mask the old man had defaced.

"Why did you do that?" he asked.

"Why did I do what?"

"Why did you pay good money for a Babylonian charm, only to vandalize it in the public square? That Phoenician could have killed you. They take their gods and demons seriously."

"Oh? The whole thing seemed kind of silly to me." The old man chuckled. The shopkeeper, too, had to laugh, partly from remembering how the old man made a fool out of the Phoenician, and partly from relief that the old man could still string a few coherent sentences together after the beating he took.

"You're hurt. He could have killed you," said the shopkeeper.

"It's true, I'm hurt," said the old man, "but you know what? It wasn't Humbaba who hurt me, was it?"

Later that night, the shopkeeper retreated to the little room in the back of his house where he kept his valuables, the finest items in his personal collection. He opened the box containing the incomplete set of figurines. Only four left. Their tiny expressionless faces stared back at him, daring him to guess what they were thinking. He handled each one carefully, trying to bring back those old feelings from childhood, but something was different. Something had changed.

"Ab? Are you back there? What are you doing?" his wife called from another part of the house. The shopkeeper lingered over the figurines a few seconds more.

"Ab?"

"I'm back here, just packing up a few items to take to the shop. I think I may be able to get a good price for them." The shopkeeper took one last look, closed the lid on the box, and joined her to help clean up the dishes from supper.

On the beaches of Phoenicia, mindless waves crept up the shore and retreated. With every advance, they brought the same rubbish onto the beach they pulled from it the time before. The rhythmic, monotonous dance, back and forth, kept an unbroken ritual, not just on the beaches of Phoenicia, but on every beach on that wild, feral globe. Yet from time to time, an item washed onshore too heavy to be swallowed back down by the ocean's titanic pull. A shell maybe, or a piece of driftwood. Or maybe an ancient clay mask with some of its teeth blacked out. These items were left for curious beachcombers, those rare individuals who care enough to look for hidden treasures, not the kind you place on a shelf, but the ones you keep in your heart to remind you there is more to life than the meaningless struggle of the waves.

The old man walked the plains of the Negeb with Abigail blithely trailing behind, the rope hanging between them with plenty of slack.

Ashes

"The Spirit of the Lord God is upon me; because the Lord hath anointed me to preach good tidings unto the meek; he hath sent me to bind up the brokenhearted, to proclaim liberty to the captives, and the opening of the prison to them that are bound; to proclaim the acceptable year of the Lord, and the day of vengeance of our God; to comfort all that mourn; to appoint unto them that mourn in Zion, to give unto them beauty for ashes, the oil of joy for mourning, the garment of praise for the spirit of heaviness; that they might be called trees of righteousness, the planting of the Lord, that he might be glorified."

Isaiah 61:1–3

The old man rose before dawn and went to the small enclosure where he kept the little red heifer. She was happy to see him, and he spoke to her softly as he looped the rope around her neck and led her out into the meadow.

He lived in the Negeb and had a long journey to make. It was nearly eighty miles to Shiloh, a four-day journey through the hill country, especially when travelling with the heifer.

"C'mon, girl," he said, tugging at the rope around her neck. "The Lord has blessed us with a beautiful morning."

He was making the long journey with the little red heifer because of a fitful dream in which his old master, now long dead, had disturbed his sleep to issue the command to make a trip to Shiloh. These nighttime visitations were common. The master couldn't just rest after being gathered to his fathers like everyone else. He considered the afterlife the perfect headquarters for sending dispatches through the dark channels of the netherworld into the old man's head. The master treated the old man the same way in death as he had in life—dispassionately and with unyielding authority. And dreams were the perfect delivery system for his demands. Before the old man could ask any questions, his master would send some terrible image—a friend missing his skin, or some foul shadow released from the depths of hell—a vision too awful to sleep through, and he would wake up before he could protest.

"Go to the house of Dathan the farmer and fetch a red heifer without blemish," the master ordered in one of these dreams. "Do not turn to the right or to the left." He wore a stern look on his face. His beard was on fire, and the old man caught a whiff of the acrid smell of burning hair.

"Take the heifer to Shiloh," the master continued, "to a place outside the sanctuary, and deliver it into the hand of the priest who is over the sacrifices. Then go your way."

"But it is the season for planting," the old man began to say. Just then the smoke began to sting his nose. At first, he thought it was his master's beard until he looked down and saw flames lapping at the hem of his garments.

He woke up, howling. His straw mattress was in flames. The lamp he kept at his bedside had fallen over and set his bed on fire. The old man smothered the flames using the corners of his bed sheets, his adrenal glands challenging the capacity of his heart muscle. When the fire was out, he rose, as if narrowly escaping death by being burned alive were a normal way to start the day.

Having acquired the heifer a few days earlier from Dathan by trading a little wheat and a few shekels of silver, the old man and Abigail—that's what he called the heifer—started their journey for Shiloh. The old man, of course, knew exactly why people carried red heifers to Shiloh, although Abigail, who was very young and naïve to the ways of the world, obviously did not.

The first day of the trip was uneventful. The old man walked the plains of the Negeb with Abigail blithely trailing behind, the rope hanging between them with plenty of slack.

They came to Beersheba late that afternoon, where one of the ancient wells of the patriarchs was. The old man smiled as he watched a group of young boys play in the meadows. The farmers had been clearing land, and where a small grove of acacia trees once stood, tall grass undulated in the wind like waves. The lilies and fennel were in bloom, and hyssop grew in thick patches here and there. The boys leaped through the fields holding sticks high above their heads in triumph while their battle cries filled the air, winning victories without fighting any wars yet, imagining spoils, not knowing their price, the bone and the blood.

The old man was sitting on the side of the well when a young girl interrupted his reveries. She stared at him with big dark eyes that looked like they might have been a better fit for a face larger and older than her own. "Would you like me to draw water for you, mister?"

"That would be very nice, and please don't forget my friend here," he said, patting the heifer.

"She's pretty. What's her name?"

"Oh, you're not supposed to name a red heifer, especially one as beautiful and perfect as this one. You could get attached."

"I see," said the girl solemnly.

"Her name's Abigail."

The girl brightened at the name of the heifer and reached out to stroke her forehead before placing a bucket of water down for her to drink.

"Are you alone?" the girl asked, turning back to the old man.

"Aside from Abigail, yes."

"Do you have any family?"

"No."

"Why not?"

"Well, child, I suppose it just wasn't the Lord's plan." The old man plunged his face into another bucket the girl had given him. After scrubbing his head and neck with the water, he sunk a finger into one of his ears down to the first knuckle and began twisting it violently while snorting loudly to clear out his sinuses. After he was satisfied he had gathered every last molecule of loose phlegm into one place, he worked it into his mouth and gave a mighty spit. He started cleaning his teeth with a twig.

"My master had a wife," he said. The tooth cleaning regimen gave him a speech impediment. "She was the most patient woman I ever met. The Lord took her when she was very young, before she had borne any children. He never got close to anyone after that. He was a good teacher, wise and always true, but he never seemed to like me. I think he was jealous of me."

"Jealous?" asked the girl. Her eyes ran a path from the old man's sandaled feet, up the camelhair cloak, over the worn leather belt, the frail chest, the wiry beard, to the blue eyes straddling a crooked nose.

"Jealous over how I never married," said the man. "I think he wished he had remained as I was."

"But didn't he love her?"

"Oh, yes, very much. But I don't think he considered love to be worth the pain that had to follow. You're too young to understand this."

"I understand," she said.

"Yes," the old man laughed, "I can see that you do. You see, it's like this. There are basically two kinds of people in this world: those who value love enough to pay its price, and those who think they want to love but feel differently when they realize how much it costs. Love is not cheap. And some don't want to pay its price. My master thought he wanted love, but when he realized how much it cost, he tried to return it. But you can't. So he made himself miserable, envying me, wishing he had never loved in the first place."

"I think love, even if you are able to be with the one you love for only a moment, is worth any price."

"We'll see, my child." He tossed the fouled water into a patch of weeds beside the well. "Thank you for your kindness. Abigail and I had best be getting on."

The prophet and the little cow headed north through the streets of Beersheba. The children skipped along beside them, petting Abigail as they passed by. Some offered her a few sprouts of alfalfa, which she gladly accepted. The adults were too busy to notice this odd procession led by the beggarly old man and his four-legged companion. The women kneading their dough hardly noticed them as they passed their kitchen windows. The farmers coming in from the fields unwittingly became temporary members of the party as it marched through the town, but each one of them broke rank with it as it passed their homes, never knowing that, as far as the children were concerned, they had been a part of history. The same indifference showed on the faces of the merchants who were packing up their wares in the marketplace, although the butcher watched the heifer as she strolled by, viewing her more in parts than as a whole cow.

The sun was going down as they reached the outskirts of Beersheba, and one by one the children abandoned the procession for home where supper awaited them, waving goodbye to the man and his red companion.

The next day they came to the hill country on the outskirts of Hebron, one of the cities of refuge. The old man was holding up as well as could be expected for a man his age. He was accustomed to hard living and felt confident that he had the strength to make the journey. His frailty did not concern him. What did concern him was that for the last several miles, he couldn't shake the feeling he was being watched. He had grown accustomed to the eyes of the

Creator on his every move, even his thoughts, but this was different. Someone followed him through the thickets of the backcountry, someone with bad intentions.

He had a general idea where his stalker was. He needed to learn his exact location so that he could keep from being ambushed and left as food for the jackals. Stopping at a little stream, he let Abigail drink while he slowly made his way around her, pretending to examine her hide to see if she had any ticks or cuts. When he came to the side of the animal opposite where he thought the stalker might be, he pretended to attend to the heifer while stealthily peering over her backbone at the brush behind them. The hill country in those parts had little vegetation, just a few scrub bushes and acacia groves, and he counted only three or four good hiding places. The old man took his time, fiddling with the cow's hide while keeping his eyes on the brush. He had narrowed the hiding places down to two possibilities.

There was movement in the brush to his left. Was that his stalker, or just a bird flapping its wings? No, the movement was too slow and cumbersome to be a bird. The old man decided to flush him out.

"All right, I know you're in there. Why don't you come out so we can get acquainted?" Nothing happened at first. The thief, or whatever he was, was either new at this, or he wasn't accustomed to someone getting the drop on him. The old man kept the heifer between himself and his follower.

"Look, I can stay here as long as you want to play this game, but sooner or later, you're going to have to come out. You've been following me for some reason. Come out and show yourself."

Larger movement in the brush indicated that whoever was in there had decided to come out and was pulling himself up to confront his quarry. A young man emerged, no more than twenty, athletic but shorter than average. He was bare chested and wore a deerskin breechcloth around his waist, and he carried a dagger strapped to his left hip. His hair was thick and black, and he showed a straight row of teeth as white as milk when he sneered.

"What do you want, son?" asked the old man, irritated that he had to be the first to speak.

"Put whatever you have of value on that rock, leave the cow, and I'll let you walk away from here with both of your arms."

"I get to keep both my arms?" the old man chuckled. "Now, that's a bargain."

"This is no joke. I've killed before, and I can kill you. You can walk away now, or I can strike you down. It makes no difference to me one way or another. Either way, I'm leaving here with your valuables and with that cow there."

The old man seemed bored, and he gazed at the sky, watching a kettle of vultures circling overhead. "I wonder who's dying?" he mused.

"You are if you don't listen, old man!" The young man was growing impatient.

"I don't have anything you want," said the old man as he continued to read the sky. "Nobody gets what they want by stealing."

"What do you know?" the young man spat. "Stealing is the only way anybody gets anything. There's more people than silver in this world, and there's no such thing as an honest rich man. You either steal, or you're stolen from. Either you take, or it's taken from you."

"And you want to be the one who takes?"

"Given the choice, I prefer taking. There's not enough to go around. Only a few people get to enjoy the good life. Why shouldn't I be one of them?"

"Everybody pays a price," said the old man. He had stepped around to the other side of the heifer so that there was no longer anything separating him from the thief.

The thief tried to mock the old man with a laugh, but it came out sounding nervous.

"Those buzzards are circling lower, dontcha think?" said the old man.

"What's it going to be, old man? You're already used up. There's not even enough meat on your bones to feed a raven. Set down your valuables and walk...."

A vulture flew just above the younger man, its talons nearly grazing the crown of his head. A black shadow crossed his face, lightless and suffocating. The bird was the only object overhead, but the shadow seemed to linger too long to have been created by its gliding wings. The shadow passed, but it left a stygian mark upon the thief's face.

The young man gagged as if he wanted to retch, and his eyes grew big and afraid. Sweat broke out on his forehead, and he quivered as if he were standing in a cold rain. He looked as if a latch had been lifted from some door in his soul, and the pitch truth of every foul deed and even every black thought he ever had were poured over him.

"I told you," said the old man, "everybody pays a price."

The old man left the thief like that on the hillside, sick and shivering, with vultures as his only companions.

It was dark by the time they reached Hebron. A sun-blistered farmer found them resting under some olive trees and invited them to stay the night. He had a short, chubby little wife who sang as she worked, and while his home was modest, it was clean, and he had plenty of food and feed for Abigail. The old man slept well, and before the sun rose the next morning, he and the heifer were heading north again to the place of the sanctuary.

They stayed in the high country and avoided the cities after they left Hebron. The old man kept the rope around the heifer, but he no longer had to pull her in the direction he wanted to go. The pair strolled side by side, making good time through the sparse hill country. The old man talked as they walked together. "People are less predictable than cows," he told Abigail. "You never know what they're going to do. Take my master. Now there's one who was hard to figure out. I was just a baby when he took me in. Never knew what happened to my mother or father—where they were from, what tribe, nothing." The old man paused for a beat to consider how he was talking to a dumb animal. But he had no one else to talk to. And, besides, Abigail was a good listener. He also had a feeling that she understood him.

"He knocked me around quite a bit when I was a kid. I guess I could be a handful. I was always getting into something. It got worse after his wife died, God rest her sweet soul. She softened him. After she was gone, every last part of him that had some give to it stove up. He became hard, unyielding. Life is stronger than we are, and if you don't bend, you break. So he broke. And I was the collateral damage. When he shattered into pieces, a few shards sliced into me. I can't say that I got past him or that I ever completely moved on. He's a part of me now, as he always has been.

"I remember this one time when I was still very young, about seven or so. She had passed a couple of years before. I remember it like yesterday. I had this little fishing net, and I had waded out into a little stream, and I was casting the net, trying to catch something. Well, you know me, Abigail, I couldn't catch a turtle, let alone a fish. But I was having fun, and he was watching me. It was just me and him, and he had this look on his face as he watched me that I had never seen before, a tender look. He even smiled, and he said, 'Come here, boy. Let me see you.' A little bewildered, but anxious as any boy would be to hear some word of approval from his father figure, I came out of the stream and sat down beside him on a log. He kept looking at me that way with that tender look on his face and smiling. He ran his fingers through my hair. He said, 'I want to tell you something, boy.' You know what he said? He said, 'I want to tell you that you will never be my son.' That's what he said: you will never be my son."

The old man stroked the heifer's forehead. "I don't need to burden you with my childhood stories," he said. "The master was good to me. He fed me and gave me a bed to sleep in when he didn't have to. He taught me the ways of the Almighty. I guess you could say I'm pretty fortunate to have known him. He will always be a part of me. Yes, he's with me now." The old man looked at the heifer with soft eyes disguised in a tangle of unmanageable eyebrows. A little more than a day, and they would be in Shiloh.

On the night before they came to Shiloh, the old man dreamed again. This time he was strolling through a wheat field, plucking the grain and rubbing it in his hands so that he could eat. Something ahead of him got his attention. First he felt the warmth on his face. Then he caught a whiff of cinders. Finally, he saw a great fire rolling through the dry tinder of the wheat at an alarming speed. There was no use in trying to escape. He could not outrun the fire, and its breadth stretched in either direction as far as his eyes could see. He braced himself, knowing that he would be burned alive, but when the fire rolled over him, he was unharmed. He felt its tremendous heat, but instead of being cooked in its scorching flames, he felt an embrace, like a mother's womb. The fire rolled past him and left nothing but ashes in its wake. Curious, the old man knelt down, scooped them up with a finger, and tasted them. The ashes were sweet to the taste. Hungry for more, he began shoveling large handfuls into his mouth, but he remained hungry. He kept gorging himself like that, scooping ashes into his face, until he woke up.

The next day they came to Shiloh. Although there was nothing unusual about seeing a man with livestock, the old man and his heifer attracted a lot of attention. Everyone they passed looked up from what they were doing to see the man in his hairy coat leading the rusty colored heifer to the sanctuary.

The priest met them at the courtyard. He was young, but he looked tired, as if he needed a break. He had a long face with a pointed chin. A cluster of warts flanked his left ear lobe, and his beard was thin and badly in need of grooming.

"I bring you this fine, red heifer," said the old man proudly. "She is without blemish, not a follicle of black hair on her. I have come all the way from the Negeb, a four-day journey, so that I might present her to the Lord's sanctuary."

The priest eyed the old man suspiciously. "Why did you do that?"

"Why, for the water for impurity, of course! A red heifer like this one is rare, indeed." The old man smiled brightly.

The priest was not impressed. "I suppose. Just put her with the other livestock in the pen over there. Peace be with you, old man."

"Wait," said the old man, "aren't you going to bless the heifer before I go? We have come all this way. It would be a shame to deposit her like trash and walk away."

The priest had already started to return to his duties and turned back around to the old man. "Do you know what we do with red heifers?"

"Yes, but…"

"We burn them. All of them. We take them outside the camp, slaughter them, and burn the skin, the flesh, the blood, and the guts. Everything!" The old man winced every time the priest emphasized each part of Abigail that was to be burned.

"A peace offering is shared with the priests. At least it is useful. But what good is a red heifer? Nothing but ashes! What a waste!"

"But it is not a waste," argued the old man. "The ashes are used to make the water of impurity for the people, so that they may be purified after becoming defiled."

"Purified? Do you really believe in all those rituals and offerings? Wake up! You are a foolish old man."

"But you are a priest!"

"Yes, I had the misfortune of being born into a family that exists for the sole purpose of providing Israel with priests. I didn't apply for the job. It was forced upon me, so here I am."

"But you are a shepherd of the people until—"

"Look, old man, all I know is that God put me on this earth to slaughter animals and burn them. That is what I have done my whole life, and that is what I'll be doing until the day I die. Now, if you don't mind, I've got several hundred animals to kill today." The priest turned without another word and walked into the courtyard to attend to his duties.

"Well, girl, I guess this is goodbye." The old man led the little red heifer to the lowing and bleating pen full of livestock waiting for their moment to atone the sins of the people, to decontaminate with blood. There were hundreds of animals, with hundreds going out and coming in every day. One after another, day after day, year after year, they were led to the slaughter by priests who sacrificed them to a righteous God who cannot bear to look upon the impurities of his sinful people.

The old man slipped the rope off the heifer's neck and took one last look, closing the gate behind him. "Lord, tell me this isn't a waste," he prayed. Then he turned his face toward his home in the Negeb, walking briskly with the empty loop of the rope swinging in his hand.

The bull bellowed and roared.

The Deepest Need

When Nathan arrived at his barn before dawn, he found the door open, sagging on its leather hinges, the heavy wooden crossbar lying in the grass several feet away.

At first he thought maybe he had forgotten to secure the barn after he had finished his work the evening before, but that was unlikely. Like all farmers, Nathan's days were described by a sequence of habits. He rarely broke the routines established in his youth, when he first started farming, laboring almost in a trance, as though he were possessed by demons. Sometimes he looked back on a plowed field or a barn full of hay at the end of the day and wondered if someone else had performed his duties while he had been sleeping.

The barn door was never opened before he arrived in the mornings.

Nathan began each day by swallowing his wife's bland gruel, drinking a half-pint of goat's milk, and grabbing a handful of dates to chew on while he covered the distance between his house and the barn to check on the one new development in his life, a prize bull he had nurtured from the time it was a calf. No event since his marriage had affected him like the birth of his bull. He marked time by it. Recent memories were now catalogued as having happened either before or after the animal burst into his dull existence.

The bull was born with a caul over his head, a rare and portentous sign, which to Nathan signified good fortune. Sadly, the mother sacrificed her life giving birth to him. She was a magnificent animal in her own right. It was as if the farm could not sustain the two of them. One had to go so the other might arrive. When she breathed her last breath, she gave her majestic spirit to her son and destined him to glory.

Now Nathan staked everything—his wealth, his family, his reputation—on the bull. If his plans worked out, he could retire early and save himself from the fate suffered by almost every farmer who dies trying to work his stubborn land with trembling hands and a crooked back. Last year alone, the bull sired forty-two calves for Nathan and the other farmers in the area. His neighbors would often drop by to covet the sleek creature skipping in Nathan's pasture, his hide dark like the space between the stars in the night sky. They noted the strength of his hindquarters, the fatal twisted grain of his black-tipped horns, his confident energy. Every farmer within a three-day journey wanted calves from Nathan's bull. A few more years of siring him out, and he would have enough money to let his farm go fallow and relax in his old age.

He approached the barn doorway slowly, stalling so that he could spend just a few more moments in a world he knew had already gone. The old mule grunted at him from inside. He peered into the darkness of the room's interior, listening for the slightest movement. The air stirred within and carried the smell of damp wood, fresh hay, leather, and animal refuse. Nathan sensed the emptiness within. He could hear the mule shifting in her stall and the goats bleating at him, trying to warn their master that his beloved routines were about to be disrupted. Nothing but silence came from the stall in the back corner.

He pulled the barn door all the way open so the morning light could shine on what he most feared and saw the empty stall. Packed straw lined the dirt floor, and the trough sat along the left side, half full of water, but the bull was gone.

Where had he gone? Could he have been stolen? Nathan thought of the eye set in velvet on the side of a head as large as a saddle. He often stared into the eye and sensed a foreign intelligence there and wondered what it took in. Did it see the same colors his eyes saw? Did it admire the heifers the way a young man notices a maiden? When that eye met his, what did it register? Did it know him? Nathan could not know the world the eye knew, but he felt it included him, recognized him, and that it was looking for him now.

Nathan hurried to the house. He slammed through the door just as his wife emerged from the shadows of the room where they slept. She discerned his uneasiness but said nothing. He ignored her and found a few unleavened cakes and some dates and shoved them into a leather satchel. Then he added an old quilted blanket.

"The bull's gone," he said, feeling the need to explain his behavior. "I think he's been stolen." His feet struck the floor heavily as he crossed the room, and his wife felt the shockwaves shudder through the small frame of the house. Nathan pulled on a hooded cloak and slung the bag over his shoulders.

"I might be away for a few days," he said.

The wife finally spoke. "Where are you going to look for him?"

"I don't know yet."

She watched him cross the floor in determined strides, and a sickening awareness fell over her face.

"You're not going to ask *him?*" she said.

"Where else can I go?" he asked bluntly. "Are *you* going to help me?"

She lowered her eyes sullenly.

"I should return in a few days," he said without looking at her and left the house, the door banging his farewell behind him.

It was early yet, and no one was on the road that wove through Nathan's village. He walked at a pace just shy of a jog. His destination lay on the other side of town, after the road faded into a path, in the scrub wilderness alongside a churning stream. It would take him the best part of a day to reach it. No one noticed him as he passed the dark butcher's shop, the cold anvil of the blacksmith, the market's empty tables. Dawn's chorus was just warming up, and the sky turned pink in the east where the sun would soon expose the world with its impartial light, impervious to bribes.

It looked like rain. The air was cool and damp, and reddish clouds rolled across the sky. Thunder sounded in the distance, and by the time he passed the last structure on the main road his cloak was damp with drizzle.

By noon the rain fell in a downpour. He had passed the last house an hour earlier. He sought shelter beneath the spare branches of an acacia and rested.

It had been raining like this the night his bull was born. He was too large for his mother to deliver him on her own, and he had to tie a rope around the calf's forefeet and pull to help her. He wasn't able to save the mother, but her new calf stood sleek and steaming in the blood-soaked straw, his head obscured by the whitish caul. When the cow looked up at her son and then dropped her heavy head with a sigh, the calf glanced at her form lying below him on the floor, milky through the membrane still covering his face, and returned to his proud pose, seemingly unphased by the death of his mother.

The rain showed no sign of letting up, and the acacia provided little shelter from the downpour, so Nathan returned to his journey, chewing on the soggy unleavened bread as he went. He needed to hurry. The more time that passed, the less chance he had of finding his bull.

He entered the scrub six hours after having cleared the town. The rain had let up, and the swollen stream directed him through the unbroken wilderness to its banks. When he reached the water, he followed it downstream, looking for the old man's house. A high white wall rose up on the other side of the ravine cut by the patient waters and tracked the stream as it cut its crooked way through the wilderness, a strange, inhuman way no man would cut, following the mysterious architecture of God. Nathan knelt on its banks and slaked his thirst in long, greedy gulps, and he could taste the silt from the runoff caused by the recent rain.

The undergrowth made the way difficult, and he now took high, loping strides to avoid clumps of water grass and slippery rocks. He reminded himself to take care with each step, lest he slip and fall and break something. At times he had to leave the stream, the brush being too thick to navigate.

Finally, the old man's mud-walled house appeared like an apparition through the scrub. The light was too dim to see through the windows, but Nathan heard from within the discordant humming of broken vocal cords. He slowed his pace, drawing nearer, unsure whether it was better to announce his approach, or creep up to the house and surprise its host by rapping on the door. He opted for stealth, but when he finally came to the door and raised a fist to knock, it sprang inward and revealed a small old man with a long, unkempt white beard and vibrant eyes that simmered beneath long, untamable eyebrows.

The old man smiled proudly, despite the broken gate of teeth that guarded his mouth. Speaking to someone behind him, he said, "We have a guest! Just in time, too, the soup's almost ready." He surveyed Nathan's wet cloak. "Why, look at you! You're soaked from the rain, you poor devil. You must be miserable. Come in, come in, don't be shy. What's mine is yours."

Nathan surveyed the single room of the house in the orange firelight and realized this wasn't much of an offer. In the corner, stained, rumpled blankets lay on the floor where the old man must have slept. A rough table and two mismatched chairs sat in the middle of the room. Another chair rested closer to the hearth before the fire. A boiling pot hung from a spit in the stone fireplace. Cobwebs drifted in the corners of the ceiling. A shaggy hide matching the one the old man wore hung from a hook on one of the walls. A small cabinet beside it held a wash basin and a pitcher, a few scrolls, and clay jars with secret contents. Dim, evening light issued out of an open window where a raven perched, intently watching Nathan. He realized this must have been the person with whom the old man was speaking when he opened the door.

The old man didn't ask Nathan why he was wandering around in the wilderness, or why he had come. Instead, he dragged another chair to the stone hearth and invited him to sit down. "Dry out there by the fire. The soup will be ready soon."

Nathan remained on his feet. "You're very kind, but I'm in a hurry. I'm sorry I had to barge in on you like this, but I'm desperate, and I need your help."

"Nonsense, my son! Sit! Sit! You've got to tell me what you need, do you not? Why not make yourself comfortable while you tell your story? Then we'll decide whether there is need for all this hurry."

Nathan saw there was no arguing with the old man, so he sat down next to the fire while his host spooned something into a bowl out of the pot hanging over the fire. He gave Nathan the bowl and returned to the pot to make a bowl for himself. Nathan sniffed the broth. The savory steam warmed his face. A bone and dark viscera of unknown origin swam in the contents. Nathan figured it was best not to inquire about the ingredients and spooned the broth into his mouth. It was hot and savory.

The old man grunted as he dropped into the chair beside Nathan before the fire. He breathed a blessing upon their meager supper and then said, "Now why don't you tell me why you're here."

Nathan swallowed and began his explanation. "I need your help. I have a prize bull I have raised since he was a calf. He's my livelihood. More than that, a companion, I guess you could say. This morning when I visited my barn, I discovered that he had been taken."

"Taken? How do you know he hasn't simply wandered off?"

"I know my bull. He wouldn't do that."

"There's no telling what a beast would or wouldn't do."

"He's different," said Nathan, realizing how silly this might sound to his host.

He decided to a less speculative approach. "Someone had lifted the crossbar and thrown it aside into the grass. The latch on the stall had been lifted. There's no sign the animal broke free. Someone led him away."

The old man pondered this for a moment, then said, "So why have you come to me for help? I am not especially qualified to handle livestock."

"They say you know things, things hidden from normal men. That you can read a man's heart. I once heard someone say you stopped a river's current to save a child from drowning."

The old man's feathery eyebrows took flight for a moment as he considered the legends Nathan told. "People exaggerate," he said. "I'm just an old fool living in a shack in the wilderness, a scroll with enough mystery about it to make someone's creative tales more convincing when they scrawl upon it with the dark ink of conjecture."

"Maybe so, but I have nowhere to turn."

"Well, you've wasted your time turning here."

The room darkened as twilight made its usual turn. Nathan looked out the window as he considered how he might convince the old man to help him. The setting sun blazed in an aura around the raven, its black feathers on fire with the burning light. The bird cocked its head to one side as if to say, *Well, Nathan, what will you say now?* Silence passed between the two men. Nathan hesitated, unsure whether he should reveal that he had a history with the old man.

Finally, he said, "You've helped before. My wife's brother. You tried to save him."

The old man stirred his bowl with his spoon. At first Nathan wasn't sure he had heard him.

"Ah! So that's you," the old man finally said. He sat his bowl on the floor and folded his gnarled hands across his lap. "That did not work out too well as I remember."

"He died. My wife didn't want me to come. She doesn't believe in you."

"You should listen to your wife." The old man rose with effort and poked at the fire.

"Look, if it's money you want, I have a few shekels—"

"Keep your silver. You have nothing I need."

"So you're not going to help me?"

"Nay."

"You can't be serious! You mean I wasted all this time bushwhacking through the wilderness to find you? I should have known better than to ask an old fool past his prime for help."

"Now, my son, don't fault me for being old. That has nothing to do with my decision. If life goes well for you, you'll get old too."

"What's keeping you from helping me? Can't you say a prayer or go into a trance or do whatever it is you do and see if you get any answers? You could at least try!"

"I'm afraid that's not the way it works."

Nathan angrily rose from the chair, still holding the half-empty bowl of bone broth. He slammed the bowl down on the table and started for the door.

"Don't be angry, my son. There's no need to rush away. I'm afraid the wilderness around here is not very friendly after dark. There are jackals, lions, and, worse, men."

"I must search for my bull. If you can't help me, I will have to be on my way."

"Please, stay, my son, please. Trust me, you'll not get far in this place at night."

Nathan knew the old man was right. He could crash in a corner of his house for the night and be on his way by dawn. He fought a quick battle with reason in his head and finally surrendered to the offer of his host.

The old man handed him a wool blanket. It was tattered but clean. Nathan snatched it ungratefully out of his hands, stretched his own quilt upon the floor, and huddled up in the corner of the dark interior of the mud-walled shack, the firelight playing upon the ceiling. The old man spoke softly to the raven as he pitched the remnants of their supper out the window and rinsed out the bowls. Nathan felt his body relax. He became very still and watched the shadows created by the firelight morph into various shapes on the ceiling and walls. He saw a dark bovine figure bucking in the flames, from delight or anguish he knew not. His eyelids grew heavy, and eventually his consciousness succumbed to the theft of sleep as it always inexplicably does.

Nathan dreamed of an ill-defined figure, seated and unstable, its outline unsteady and out of focus. A musk, the earthy odor of hive, assaulted his nostrils, and as he drew closer, he could see that the figure was covered in hornets. A voice spoke his name—his wife's! She called him, asking him to rescue her, but when he reached out to seize her by the arm, his hand passed through the swarm, and the figure that cried out to him with the voice of his wife broke into a cloud. He turned and ran, but he could not outpace the hornets. They began to sting him on the hands, on the forearms, on his neck. They filled his eyes and nostrils, digging their way in. His lips had been closed tightly to keep them out of his mouth, but he could no longer resist the impulse to scream. He opened his mouth to cry out, but instead of screaming he swallowed a swarm of angry hornets. They tunneled into his core. He felt a presence within him, another consciousness knowing him, reading his secrets. Panic gripped his heart. He ran, trying to flee the presence within him, but he slammed into a hard wall. He found that he was blind, or in pitch darkness. The other consciousness was still there, seeing everything. He was naked and vulnerable. He ran in the other direction and hit another wall. Trapped, he wailed a futile cry and then—

"Wake up." The old man stood over him, speaking. "We need to get an early start if we're going to find your bull."

Nathan rubbed his eyes. "But last night you said you weren't going to help me."

"I changed my mind" was all the old man said.

"So where're we headed?" Nathan interrogated the old man as they high-stepped the rocky terrain marked by desert scrub, tall grasses, and acacia and broom trees. The raven flew ahead of them, lighting from tree to tree in the cool morning air.

"We're heading through the village on the main road and then east toward the highland."

"That's where I live!" exclaimed Nathan. "He must not be far from home."

The old man made no further comment.

After an hour of fighting the unmarked wilderness, they came to the faint path that would eventually become the road into town. The old man stopped, pulled a water skin from his satchel, and drank. Nathan stood impatiently beside him, too eager for rest.

The lack of activity gave his mind time to wander back to those early days when the bull skipped through his pasture. He spent hours leaning on the fence, watching him play for the sheer pleasure of it. His wife accused him of treating the animal as if it were his own son. "You have given up on a family," she said. "Shall I set a place for it at our table?" He told her to stop nagging him. If the Lord wanted them to have children, they would have children. And so what if he took pride in his bull? Had he not delivered him with his own hands? Had he not stood in for his mother, feeding him milk a drop at a time until he reached the age of weaning? He could not help it if she had been jealous. He had not robbed her of the ability to have children. Was he God? Why did she always seem to blame him? He couldn't give her children, but he could secure for them a future. That is, if he could find the bull.

"Let's go," said Nathan to the old man, "we don't have all day."

By noon they approached the garrison on the outskirts of the village. The day before, Nathan passed it before the soldier reported for the morning watch, but today a young man stood roadside, a sword strapped to his left hip. Bored by another uneventful day and eager for diversion, even one of his own making, he thrust out a hand toward the approaching men in a signal that read *Stop. Explain yourselves.* The men drew up next to the garrison.

The soldier recognized Nathan and gave him a friendly greeting. "Hello Nathan! What brings you from that direction this time of the day?"

Wishing to avoid any interference by the authorities, Nathan gave a clipped explanation. "My friend here lives out that way, in the wilderness. He's assisting me with a personal matter."

"Personal matter?" The soldier lifted his chin and squinted at the old man, examining him carefully.

"Yes, I see no need to bore you with the details. Just some business with livestock."

The soldier spoke to Nathan without taking his eyes off the old man. "How's your bull? I hear he's a magnificent animal."

"Yes, he's a fine bull." Nathan tried to smile and said, "Well, if you'll excuse us—"

"Wait just a minute." The soldier wasn't finished. "You said this old fella lives in the wilderness?"

"Yes—"

"He wouldn't be the old man who got your wife's brother killed, would he?"

If the soldier's recognition disturbed the old man, it didn't show. He turned to Nathan to see how he would respond.

"That was just a misunderstanding—"

"Misunderstanding, I'll say!" mocked the soldier. "He's supposed to be this miracle worker, they say. Dreams of the future, makes time stand still." The soldier snorted. "Turns out he's just a dried-up old cow chip who gives people false hope. I'd chain him up to see what he might do, but there wouldn't be any fun in it. On your way, miracle worker! Go break some more promises for that silly fool!"

"C'mon," said Nathan, pulling the old man past the garrison by the arm. The old man smiled at the soldier as they departed.

"Sorry about that," said Nathan after they put some distance between themselves and the garrison. "He doesn't know what he's talking about."

They were now on the main road through town. Nathan could feel the eyes of the men, scrutinizing his intentions. He heard the women's whispers, the children's muffled giggles. He quickened his pace and focused on getting to the other side of town and finding his bull.

"Maybe I should go back," said the old man suddenly.

"What do you mean? You said you knew where my bull was. Why should we quit now?"

Unlike Nathan who kept his head down, the old man swiveled his head, surveying the town's reaction to their presence on the street. Every head that met his gaze quickly shifted to another direction.

"This animal may be more trouble than he's worth," suggested the old man.

"Nathan stopped in the street and turned to face the old man. "Look," he explained, "this isn't just any bull. This is everything. My future! I can make enough money from that bull to live on for the rest of my life. I've been waiting for an animal like this my whole life."

"Silver has very little to do with happiness."

"It's not just the money," said Nathan, brushing off the old man's words. "He's special. We have this—connection." Nathan thought of the clear dark dome of the incommunicable eye, where a chartless conscious lived, unknowable but knowing, as aware of him as he was it. "I must find him," he said, his voice quavering.

The old man stooped down, picked up a smooth stone, and rolled it in his hand. "Maybe you want to find him, maybe you're looking for something else," he said casually while studying the stone.

"What do you mean by that? What else would I be looking for?"

"I'm simply saying that few men consider the need—the deeper need—before they start looking for what they think they want. I will help you, but first I will ask you to ponder carefully your need. Not your felt need—your feelings are prone to betrayal. Your deeper desires. Lungs gasp for air, the stomach growls for food, the tongue thirsts for water, the bed for a woman. But your soul? What does your soul long for? A bull? Will you sell your soul to a beast? Think carefully, my son, is that your soul's deepest need?"

Nathan knew he should be patient with the old man. After all, he had dragged him from his home on this mission, appealing to his sense of duty while offering nothing in return. But he grew weary of the old man's hesitation. He knew where his bull was, Nathan was sure of it. The bull belonged to him. Someone had stolen it. The old man could help him find what was rightfully his. Was that not enough reason to go looking for it?

Nathan summoned his self-control and sighed. "Why does this have to be about my deepest need, old man? Can we not search for what is rightfully mine without making it my soul's foremost desire?"

The old man pressed his lips together and looked Nathan in the eye. "I just need to know this is what you really want."

"Yes! This is what I want, okay?" Nathan had raised his voice and attracted more attention. A group of women along the road stopped their chatting and looked in unison at the pair like a herd of deer snapping their heads in the direction of the sound of a broken twig and bracing their hind legs for flight.

"So. Let us hasten before the sun grows dim," said the old man.

An hour later the two men stood within twenty feet of the bull. It munched on a pile of hay on the other side of a split rail fence. Not far away, a pile of brush and deadwood smoldered. The smoke blew in the direction of the two men, cloaking the scene in a suffocating cloud bespeaking judgment.

"I don't believe it!" exclaimed Nathan pacing back and forth along the fence while holding the sides of his head. "Javan has been my neighbor for more than twelve years!"

The bull watched Nathan tiredly as he munched on the hay, as if he had witnessed the tedious routine of Nathan's outbursts before.

"Don't jump to conclusions," urged the old man.

"I'm not jumping to conclusions! Javan stole my bull! What else could it be?" Nathan's pace quickened, and his face reddened as he pictured his supposed friend breaking into his barn.

"Maybe your bull wandered off and Javan discovered him and secured him here until he was able to notify you or return him. That is just what the law requires."

"No!" cried Nathan, "He stole him! He snuck into my barn and took him!"

The old man stepped in front of Nathan and stopped his pacing. "Think about it," he reasoned. "He would never get away with it. How do you hide a bull like that?"

"No one ever accused Javan of having a whole lot of sense," said Nathan. He had stopped looking at the old man and was peering over his shoulder at the brushfire.

"Nathan?" said the old man, trying unsuccessfully to regain the other man's attention. "What are you thinking?" It was uncertain whether the old man could really read minds, but one thing was certain—Nathan's was inscrutable to him now.

The bull had stopped munching and seemed to wait with the old man for his master's answer. An old, rotten barn leaned to one side about fifty yards away, and Nathan kept looking from it to the brushfire and back again.

"I'm going to get what I need, old man."

Nathan strode to the smoldering brush and pulled out a firebrand. In one smooth action, he tossed it into the loft where Javan stored his hay. Despite its looks, the barn had kept the hay dry from the rain that had fallen the previous day. The men heard a low whoosh of combustion, and an orange glow lit the top level of the barn.

"What have you done?" cried the old man. If Nathan heard him, he didn't show it. His hard, expressionless face locked onto the barn. A fire as intense as the one consuming Javan's barn had overtaken his senses, one burning with vengeance and outrage, yet untouched by the ramifications of what he had done.

The old man ran to the house to fetch Javan.

The bull, alarmed by the flames and the black smoke churning from the barn, grew agitated and snorted and pawed at the ground. His eyes, once round and dark, now narrowed, reddened with the reflection of fire.

Nathan ran to the gate at the entrance of Javan's pasture and lifted the leather loop that secured it to the rail.

He approached the animal slowly with arms outstretched, speaking gently to calm him. "Easy, fella, you're alright. I'm going to take you home."

The bull lowered its head and snorted and pawed at the ground, drawing up dust so that it appeared that the ground too had begun to smolder with fire. His black coat shone with perspiration, and his shoulders flexed with aggression.

"Easy!" Nathan realized he had been shouting at the bull the way he had been yelling at the old man. He tried a smile and calmed his voice. "It's just me, Nathan, your old friend. I've cared for you your whole life. Nothing's going to happen to you. It's all over. We're going home."

"Nathan!" Shouts came from the direction of Javan's house. Taking his attention away from the bull, Nathan squinted against the sting of the acrid air and saw two men running toward him through the billowing clouds of smoke.

He grinned maliciously and shouted in their direction. "You won't get away with this!"

A low droning rushed from behind him. Turning, he saw that the noise came from thousands of tiny wings. A swarm of angry hornets had flown out of the burning barn toward him. Stings pricked his skin, and another fire, the fire of blind pheromonal fury, set his arms and neck aflame.

The bull bellowed and roared. Nathan turned his attention back to his beast and saw the hornets swarming around its nose and eyes. He fought the pain and tried to form a few familiar, soothing words, but his lips were too swollen by the hornet's stings to speak decipherable sounds, and he could not raise his voice above the thrashing and wailing of the bull.

Then something belted him in the stomach and knocked out his breath. He felt an icy stabbing sensation in his core. His hands instinctively dropped to cover the part of his body where he had felt the impact, but instead of feeling the garments that wrapped around his middle, he felt the warm, sweaty hide of his bull. He realized the horizon was moving swiftly down and to the left, and then his body pitched forward. A wind blew in his face, and he saw the back of the bull pass under him. Another impact, this time more jarring, shook his entire frame. He felt his teeth bite through his tongue, and the ground skinned his elbows and knees. A sickening gasp came from somewhere, and when he tried to call out to the old man, he realized the sound had come from his own lungs. His head ached from the black air. His body lay contorted, a red pool spread from underneath him. He had been gored by the bull.

The old man led the bull on a limp rope down the road from Javan's place to the adjacent farm. The bull followed complacently, the air weary raven on his back, judging the world indiscriminately from his perch, interested only in what was natural and true, a world stripped of interpretation. They drew up to the house belonging to the next farm and waited. Presently, a woman bundled in a wool blanket shuffled out into the rosing light of the dying day to meet them in the road.

"So he found you, then," she said.

"I'm returning your bull," said the old man.

Her eyes moved from the dried blood on one of the animal's horns to the dark eye, round and clear again, no longer filled with panic and fire, empty of remorse. She frowned and snapped her head in the old man's direction.

"Where's Nathan?" she asked.

"Your husband's dead," the old man said bluntly.

The woman could not hold his gaze. She looked to the raven for support, but the bird cocked its head as if waiting for an answer.

"Have you ever helped anyone who hasn't wound up dead?" she asked bitterly.

It was now the old man's turn to avert his eyes.

"This is why I begged him not to find you. Everyone speaks of you as if you are an angel, some kind of a miracle worker. You're an angel all right, an angel of death!" Her voice was sharp and bitter, and she forcefully wiped a tear from her eye. "You have some nerve coming here like this, with that beast. Why won't you leave me alone?"

"The animal belongs to you. Someone let him out yesterday morning, and he wandered into Javan's pasture. But I think you already knew that."

Nathan's wife looked away toward the sun setting on the horizon.

"I didn't mean for it to come to this," she said. She shivered and gathered the blanket around her shoulders. "He spent so much time with that beast! I had to do everything myself. I was losing my mind! We never spoke unless it was about that animal. He called it our future. 'We'll never have another worry,' he said. He was obsessed! I had to do something, you see? I just wanted it out of our lives, so he would see me again! I never meant for him to ..."

The woman's words broke into sobs. She wept without shame, as if she were alone. The old man had disappeared as far as she was concerned.

The old man pressed his lips together and looked toward the east. The setting sun bathed his beard in vengeful light. "The animal will have to be destroyed," he said. "It is the law."

The bull registered no reaction to the news of his demise. He lowered his head and grazed on the sparse grass along the roadside.

"I don't care," the woman sobbed. "Good! See to it yourself. I don't want him. Take him away. I don't ever want to see him again."

"So. Peace be with you."

Taking flight, the raven led the old man and the docile bull back toward Javan's farm, where the animal's blood would join his master's. Its shadow merged with the old man's to form a stretched out chimera on the road, while the raven's black ill-shapen form punctuated the picture on the road behind them.

His fingers gripped the hull, and he rested, panting and hanging on for dear life.

Burden

Caleb lived in dread of falling asleep. He rarely slept until dawn before some black shade shuddered him awake in a twisted mess of damp sheets, although he really couldn't blame the nightmares. He woke himself up with his own screams, prolonged, transient screams that climbed out of the depths of his subconscious into the real world.

His wife left him years ago. "It makes no sense for both of us to lose sleep every night," she said. She had become as anxious about going to bed as Caleb. She complained that he made her heart leap out of her chest every night, waking her up screaming like an evil spirit and flailing at her with clinched fists while fighting the monsters in his ghastly dreams. One night, Caleb awoke with his hands around her throat. He felt sick every time he thought about her gasping for breath while he shook her by the neck. He begged her to forgive him, explaining that he had been caught up in some dreamy trance, convinced she was some threat to his safety instead of his wife. That was their last night together. The next day, she packed her bags and went home to her mother and father. Maybe it was for the best. She would die childless, but at least she would not die choking in the grip of her maniac husband.

Caleb's wife was not the only one who noticed his problem. On more than one occasion, concerned pedestrians passing by his window in the early morning rapped at his door until he came and assured them, embarrassed, that he suffered from night terrors and that, no, he had not been attacked by a thief who had broken into his home, beaten him senseless, and stolen his money.

His dreams were recurring, and they were always nightmares. In the latest iteration, he dreamed that a tower held the sky like a solitary pillar supporting the world, and he was trapped in some vast, hellish cellar underneath. He could not see the real world's blue skies, buzzing commerce, and people. He could not see families or hear laughter. He could not smell the aroma of freshly baked bread or hear the sea lapping at the shore. All he could see was the cloudy, grey underbelly of a life far away.

He felt heat radiating through his sandals. Where was he? In every direction he saw nothing but a lifeless, ashy landscape. No vegetation, no animals, no people, not even a cockroach. Hot wind chapped his lips and burned his cheeks. The air was full of stinging grit. He blinked and tried to clear his vision, but he only made matters worse because the debris or gravel or whatever it was scratched his eyes when he rubbed them.

He squinted upwards, but he couldn't see the top of the tower. It stretched for what seemed like miles into the sky. No windows or supporting structures surrounded it. From the outside, it looked like a perfect cylinder, bolting straight up from its foundations. He stared at its smooth walls, amazed. The builders, whoever they were, must have constructed it from the inside, working their way up using scaffolding and staircases.

The tower was impressive. It held the whole world, but Caleb couldn't shake the thought that something wasn't right. He felt a sinking, hopeless feeling instead of admiration. He couldn't explain why, but the looming tower filled his heart with disappointment. Something was all wrong, like maybe it shouldn't have been there. Maybe *he* shouldn't be there. Who had thrown him into this flimsy netherworld?

Caleb didn't know where to go or what to do. He looked around, trying to find a sign or a road or someone he could ask. A bolted door sat silently at the base of the tower. He tried pulling on its heavy ring in vain and then used it to knock against the thick wood. Silence. He tried again, knowing no one would answer. Was he stuck outside this tower, alone? Why was he there? He licked his parched lips with a thirsty tongue. If he didn't find help soon, he would die out here.

Suddenly Caleb's blood ran cold, and gooseflesh crawled up his arms and on the back of his neck. Even though he could see for miles in every direction, and he had taken a good look around before knocking on the door, he felt a pair of tired eyes searching him. Yes, someone was standing close behind him. He turned to see a frail old woman, smiling, in a black hooded cloak. He saw the two smooth pink rims of her gums.

"Where did you come from?" he asked in surprise.

She opened her mouth to speak, but he never heard what she said because at the same time, thunder rolled overhead. Or was it the tower?

The ground began to quake. The woman turned to go, still smiling. She waved over her stooped shoulders as she walked away into the endless hellscape.

"Wait!" he cried. "Come back! Where am I? What's happening?" He begged her desperately to help him until he realized he couldn't see her anymore. She vanished as quickly as she appeared.

Then dust and debris began falling from the sky, followed by stones and chunks of mortar. He realized it was coming from the tower. The pieces started falling more frequently and in greater amounts, and he could see the whole tower swaying back and forth. He desperately looked for shelter, but there was nowhere to hide.

Other things started falling—bundles of grain, wagons, pieces of silver and gold, barrels of wine, chairs, and tools. He watched a doll made of corn silk fall. Then he heard the bleating of sheep and the lowing of cattle. Animals fell, their bodies hitting the ground with a tremendous thud. Then came men, women, and children. Babies.

He watched all this, wishing something would drop on him and kill him so he did not have to witness the falling objects, but somehow, he was spared. The ground shook under his feet with each stone, each body, each piece of the tower, but it all fell around him in piles, never on him.

Finally, the tower collapsed sending shockwaves that made the ground buck and toss, and then he woke up.

If these visions had only been a phase, he might have been able to endure them, but they had been plaguing him for years now. Their permanence had an isolating effect on him, shoving him into a chink between his own private dreamworld and his waking life, never fully a part of one or the other, always the guest, never at home.

And that was not all. As if the restless nights and the terror were not enough, Caleb also had to deal with an accompanying impulse to speak the dreams. At some point he discovered that he could get a recurring vision to stop harassing him by introducing it to the waking world, as one would arrange a meeting between friends from two separate parts of life. But these introductions got him into trouble. They always left Caleb wishing he had kept his mouth shut—even if it meant pinning his jaws together or cutting out his tongue.

People didn't like his dreams, especially those who held positions of power. The priest, who was most annoyed by them, reported his concerns about the "troublemaker"—that was his pet name for Caleb—to the king. Without the priest there to interpret Caleb's visions, the king might have been too dense to understand them as anything more than the absurd ravings of a madman. But the priest was as intelligent as he was dangerous. He detected insurrection and accusations of corruption behind the troublemaker's wild nightmares and flavored his reports of Caleb's public addresses with these interpretations. Then it was the stocks for Caleb, or the whip, or solitary confinement, without due process or proper judicial proceedings. No trial, no witnesses, just immediate punishment, the sentence determined by the priest alone.

Caleb hated the priest, but the dark clouds of the injustices he suffered had a silver lining because in the king's dungeon, sleeping on the cold, damp, stone floor, Caleb finally rested. He made up for months of sleep deprivation in prison, sleeping twelve or more hours at a time. During one period of confinement, he missed an entire day and awoke, expecting to see blue skies out his window but finding instead, to his surprise, the darkness of early morning the day after. These moments of respite were short-lived though, and the cycle repeated itself with a new nighttime specter that kept him tossing and sweating every night.

Caleb knew a way out. He had been hesitant to try it because he had acquired this information from a forbidden source, the enchantress who lived in the woods. Nobody knew how old she was, and she claimed she could speak with the dead, which was unlawful. Caleb visited her on an impulse in a moment of weakness, and she taught him how to suppress his dreams. However, by the time he arrived home he decided not to follow her advice. Better to face the threats of dreamy apparitions and corrupt public officials than the wrath of God.

One morning, however, after a long night of tossing and turning, Caleb awoke, breathing hard, his heart racing, and his throat sore from screaming. Frustrated, he threw off his blankets, rolled off the pallet, and tried to stand, but a thudding commenced in his head, and a black curtain began to close, so he lay back down until he could recover. He lay there thinking he couldn't live like this anymore. He had to take matters into his own hands. Nobody was going to save him. Caleb had to face his problem alone. His parents were dead, his wife had left him, and the priest threw him into prison. Not even God pitied him.

He had prayed for peace and asked God to release him, but still the dreams plagued him. Why did he have to dream these dreams? He couldn't remember signing a contract. He felt more like a tool than a person. That's all he was—a hammer to beat the king's head. But he was too soft to be God's hammer. He was more lead than iron, misshapen by the blows. The sages said even the lowest sinner could turn to God, no matter what they had done. Even after one's own mother turns her back on him, he still had God. At least that is what they said. But God wasn't answering Caleb's prayers. He would have to solve this problem alone. Forbidden or not, he decided to use the secret he learned from the enchantress.

Caleb dressed and ate a breakfast of dates and stale bread and set out for the docks. A storm had swept the sky clean the night before, and it was a bright morning. Songbirds accompanied children's laughter, and several couples strolled arm in arm along the streets surrounding the city. Caleb walked with them, but he wasn't really there. He was like an apparition whose true home was at the base of the crumbling tower. Every dream was like that with Caleb. He carried them like a burden. He could speak them, and they would depart for a time, but he wasn't going to do that anymore. No way. He would rather live the rest of his life in the shadow of the looming tower with rocks and plaster and cows showering around him than speak. Let someone else be God's hammer, he thought. Let them whip someone else and throw him into a pit or put his feet in stocks.

He passed the city gates and saw the elders putting another poor family out of their home. He stopped for a moment and fell in with the crowd of witnesses who were watching the proceedings. The elders sat on a platform under a canopy in the cobblestone courtyard between the outer gate and the inner gate of the city. Before them stood a rich landowner on one side and a farmer in shabby clothing on the other, who no doubt owed the other man money. Looks like someone's about to acquire some more free labor, Caleb thought to himself. The trial was a sham. Caleb knew the landowner had greased the elders' pockets before the trial began. The farmer didn't stand a chance, and he knew it. He spoke only when ordered and stood there waiting for it to happen. His tired arms hung by the threads of his shoulders as his eyes followed a fly jumping off a piece of rotten fruit lying in the courtyard. The farmer's wife and children stared at the proceedings with empty eyes. Everyone knew it was a sham. The people had come to accept injustice as a way of life, just another inconvenience like not having enough rain or having to eat when hungry.

Caleb walked on, leaving the city leaders to their dirty work. He followed the city wall for a mile or so. When the docks came into view, he followed the gentle slope toward the sea. The breeze picked up, and his ears filled with the sounds of the waves and gulls crying. Most of the boats were out for the day. He could see a few on the horizon, and the docks were almost empty. He knew, however, that the fisherman would be there. He always worked at night. Caleb expected to find him packing his gear and getting ready to go home to his wife, a hot breakfast, and a comfortable bed.

He found the dock he was seeking and strolled down its boarded planks to the boat. He caught the fisherman straddling the bow while rolling up some of the rigging he used for fishing. He was stripped to the waist, and his big brown shoulders shimmered and rolled in the morning sun. The boat rocked in rhythm with the waves, squeaking against the dock, the primal friction of motion and inertia.

"Got any leftovers today?" Caleb asked.

"What's that?" the fisherman asked.

"Leftovers. You know, scraps of fish or bait you couldn't use?" Caleb stepped lightly into the boat and looked into one of the barrels lashed onto the gunwale.

"What do you want with that?" the fisherman asked.

"That's my business. Do you have any or not?"

The fisherman studied Caleb for a beat. "Sure. Just give me a second," he said. He finished rolling up the rigging and stepped off the bow. He fetched a bucket from the stern and handed it to Caleb. Flies buzzed excitedly around the opening, and a warm smell of decay came from inside. "I'm through with it anyhow."

"Thanks," said Caleb, turning to go.

"Is everything all right?" asked the fisherman. "You don't look so good."

"I'm fine. Don't worry about it," answered Caleb.

"Hey, I want my bucket back."

"I'll be back for a refill," said Caleb, who hopped out of the boat and strode briskly down the dock. When he reached the end, he looked back and saw the fisherman still watching him. He returned a wave and headed back toward the city.

As he walked home, Caleb inspected his catch of the day. Inside the bucket, several lidless eyes stared back at him. The bucket was full of fish heads, tails, fins, and guts. More than enough, he thought.

He walked home quickly, trying not to attract attention, although this was hard because while he might have been able to avoid being seen, there was nothing he could do about the smell. Everyone he passed on the streets followed him with their eyes, watching especially the fly-infested bucket swinging by his side. They whispered to one another with nauseated looks on their faces as he walked past them. Caleb didn't care what they thought. He just wanted to be left alone when he was awake and when he was asleep.

When he reached home, he walked out to the field behind his house, his eyes carefully examining the grass. Finally, he found what he was looking for, gathered a bunch in his hands, and went into the house.

Inside, he ground some of the wormwood and hyssop together with a little garlic. This he set aside. He scooped a handful of fish parts out of the bucket, set them on the table, and covered them with a cloth. Then he beat the fish with a stone into a thick pulp. Caleb lifted the cloth to inspect his work. The fish had become a smelly, white, gelatinous lump. He fought for control as his stomach turned a notch, and his eyes watered. He added the garlic, herbs, fish, and a little water into a bowl and stirred the ingredients until they were thoroughly mixed. Then he took a deep breath and raised the bowl to his lips. His hands shook as he tipped the bowl back, and the thick, noxious mixture rolled into his mouth. Despite his best efforts to pulverize the fish, it still had a lumpy texture. He could feel bones raking his throat as the potion slid down to his stomach. Caleb swallowed hard. He gagged, but he kept everything down.

Caleb lay down on his pallet. The mixture sat on his stomach like a stone. It made him ill, but he welcomed the nausea. Rotten fish was a fitting meal for a pitiful fool. He lay there alone, sick and sweating, but he could sleep. And he would not dream.

For several weeks, Caleb returned to the docks for more fish, and each time the puzzled fisherman complied with his request for his leftover bait.

One morning, however, the fisherman changed the routine. "I'll give you this delicious, steaming bucket of guts on one condition," he said, "that you accompany me on my run tonight."

Caleb's shoulders slumped, and his face twisted into a look of agony.

"Oh, c'mon! It won't be that bad! I could use the company, and the water will do you good."

"Can't you just give me the fish?"

"No, this is not negotiable. Either go out with me tonight or go home emptyhanded."

Caleb thought about this for a moment, then leaped from the dock into the boat, resigned to his fate.

"I'll just set this here. This boat is smelly enough as it is," the fisherman said, reaching over the hull and setting the bucket of fish scraps onto the dock. "They won't go anywhere."

"I get seasick," Caleb warned. Truthfully, he was sick every day, something he feared his pale, sweaty complexion made obvious to the fisherman. His questions and concern made Caleb uncomfortable.

"You'll get used to it," the fisherman said while hauling anchor and setting sail. "I have a feeling we're going to get lucky tonight."

There was just enough light left in the evening sky for Caleb to make out three clouds scarcely larger than his hand over the hills to the east. The water lay before them smooth as glass, and the fisherman's expert hand guided the rudder's blade as it cut its way toward the depths, where the fish were waiting.

Caleb had to admit that the water was good for him. Out here on the sea, there were no ears besides his and the fisherman's. No one to debate and argue with. No one to curse and be cursed. No priest to shove him and slap his face to shut him up.

The fisherman was a good listener. He didn't seem opinionated, except when it came to good fishing spots and Caleb's mental health. He didn't seem to care about politics or religion. Out here away from the city, cut off from the land, a man had a chance to mend, which might have explained the certainty in the fisherman's movements and the kindness in his eyes.

The fisherman placed Caleb at the oars while he manned the tiller. The oars pulled hard against the tholepins, straining Caleb's back with every stroke. Caleb enjoyed concentrating solely upon their movement—pulling them back against the sea's heavy waters, lifting the dripping paddles out of the waves, pushing them forward, and plunging them in again, repeating the cycle. The rhythm of rowing had a meditative effect upon him. He knew he'd be sore the next day, but he liked the feeling of the night air blowing on his face. Something tight inside him opened slightly, just enough for him to feel it, but not enough to release the burden. It still lay coiled, sleeping within him, drunk with the potion, but alive, waiting for him to relax, and then it would pounce. No matter how sick it made him, no matter how heavy the burden, he would hold it in. He would not speak.

The fisherman opened the lateen sail and aimed the rudder toward his usual location, about fifteen to twenty miles offshore. They reached their destination at about first watch. The fisherman fetched a large casting net from the stern and checked every square inch for tears needing mending. This was unnecessary, since he had inspected his nets the day before, but years of fishing had taught him certain habits he could not escape, no matter how unnecessary or time consuming they were.

"Drop those drift anchors overboard," he ordered. Caleb would not have known who he was talking to if he had not been the only other man in the boat. The fisherman was a different man on the sea than he was on the docks. Fishing was serious business, and he did not have time now for idle chat or pleasantries.

The fisherman tossed the round casting net overboard. While he waited for the weights on the head rope to drift to the sea floor, he stripped off his clothes. After he had given the net its time, he dove in to retrieve it, completely disappearing out of sight longer than it seemed a man without gills could stand. Eventually, he emerged with a flopping net. He climbed into the boat, sorted out the tilapia, and cast the unwanted specimens into the water. Then he repeated this ritual again and again, so many times Caleb lost count. Caleb understood now why the fisherman seemed impatient with him sometimes. The work was exhausting, but it was profitable, and after several hours the boat was hopping with fish.

"Don't you think we have enough?" Caleb asked.

"We've still got a little time till morning. Let's stay out a few more hours."

Caleb stretched and rubbed his shoulders. He felt good earlier, but the bile was starting to rise in that familiar way, and he felt like he might throw up.

"Is it just me or is the water getting choppy?" asked Caleb.

"It's fine," said the fisherman, sitting down next to Caleb for a breather. He was still naked, and Caleb felt uncomfortable.

"What do you do with all those rotten heads and guts anyway?" the fisherman asked suddenly.

"Why do you care?"

"I don't know. It's strange. There's no use for them. I'm curious."

"I'd rather not say."

"Fine by me," said the fisherman. "I'd just throw them away if I wasn't keeping them for you. It doesn't matter to me who eats them, whether it's a catfish or some crazy fool."

"I'm not crazy," said Caleb.

"What are you doing to yourself, Caleb? You're always alone, doing God knows what in that shack outside of town. You look like death warmed over. You don't take care of yourself or wash your clothes."

"At least I'm wearing clothes."

"I'm working." said the fisherman, enjoying Caleb's embarrassment. "Besides, you're naked too. You just don't know it."

"What?" said Caleb, self-consciously pulling the collar of his tunic closed.

“I see right through you, Caleb. You think you have everybody fooled. Think you’re hiding out, but I see you. I know what you’re up to.”

“And what’s that?” Caleb asked. He tried to make his voice sound puzzled when he posed this question, but it came out sounding like someone trying too hard to sound clueless. He knew the fisherman could see him. Caleb always grumbled about being alone, about how nobody cared. Why was he so evasive now that someone showed a genuine interest in him?

“You don’t know me,” Caleb said. “No one does. So let’s just finish up and sail back to shore.”

“I know more than you think,” the fisherman said, pulling on his tunic. “My grandfather was like you. He saw things, visions. My parents hated it when he told me his dreams. He embarrassed them, and they were afraid he might influence me.

“One day, on my way home from playing in the fields, I heard shouting coming from the house. My father was yelling at him. ‘I don’t ever want to see you again,’ he said. ‘You’re a disgrace!’ That was the last time I saw my grandfather.

“Whether it was real or not, he saw things others couldn’t understand. They *wouldn’t* understand. Fantastic things. Frightening things. He made them uncomfortable, so they sent him away to die somewhere alone. I don’t even know if he received a decent burial.

“I couldn’t help him. But I can help you if you will just talk to me. You don’t have to wind up like him.”

“I won’t wind up like him. I’ve made sure of that,” Caleb said.

“How’s that? By poisoning yourself with rotten gills and guts and God knows what else?”

Caleb watched the moon’s curved white leg skip along the waves. “People speak of truth as if it were royalty riding on our shoulders, as if it would be an honor to carry it. I’ll tell you what the truth really is. It’s something nobody really wants to hear.

Truth is nightmare. We try to lock it away in dark corners so we can ignore it, but if we sit still long enough, it breaks free and haunts the deep chambers of our minds.

"You speak with a friend. You keep the conversation away from anything important, talk about taxes, games, construction, whatever. Your friend leaves, and you are alone. Then truth spreads its awful wings and casts a shadow over your trivial thoughts.

"Or you lie down to sleep because you must. Think about it! The perfect man would not have to rest, but God built a flaw in us, the need for sleep. So we must lie down every night in darkness, without our dear distractions, alone with our thoughts. Then truth comes to us in our dreams.

"We speak nobly of truth, but we cower in fear when it visits. Nobody really cares about the truth. I'll tell you what truth is. It's not royalty. It's not a gift. It's a burden."

"You can't mean that!" said the fisherman. "Truth is reality. It's the way things are, whether we accept it or not. Caleb, you are a rare specimen. These dreams—they reveal what's real! Nothing is more important than that! Don't you see?

"Besides, you can't deny your calling. You're a dreamer. That's who you are. And dead fish aren't going to change that. The dreams haven't gone anywhere. You just haven't had them in a while because you haven't been sleeping! Eventually, you will have to sleep, and they will return."

"Not if I can help it," said Caleb.

"You know something?" The fisherman spoke to Caleb's profile as his face stubbornly focused on the sea. "I don't think you really eat those fish parts to suppress your dreams. I think you're punishing yourself. You've received visions, but you'd rather believe a petty priest who is only interested in silver and power. He tells you you're nothing, and you believe him, so you make yourself sick!

"Look, Caleb, the people are suffering. You can help them, and they will support you. I will support you. You don't have to die alone."

Caleb turned to the fisherman. "Look, I'm fine, okay? I'm not going to die alone. I am going to throw up, though, so can we please go ashore?"

The fisherman sighed and slapped his thighs. "Whatever you say."

The fisherman stood and noticed that while they had been talking, the wind had picked up and the boat had begun to rock. A gale blew in from the northeast, too forceful to risk hoisting the sail.

Taking the oars, the fisherman said, "We had better head for the nearest lee and wait this out. It doesn't look like we are going to have enough time to reach home before this gets bad." But within minutes, a howling wind nearly picked the men off their feet. Powerful gusts funneled through deep gorges and struck the lake with an incredible force. Torrents of rain fell in sheets. Waves picked them up and slung them down, leaving the men dizzy and disoriented. The change came suddenly, as if their boat had somehow transported itself from a clear evening in summer to a fierce rainstorm in the spring of the next year.

It was impossible to determine which way the wind was blowing. The battling gusts churned the water in every direction so that the boat tossed this way and that. Caleb, whose stomach had already been challenging his ability to hold down his supper, finally succumbed to the boat's maniacal rocking, leaned over the gunwale, and retched. He fought to hold onto consciousness. The blackness wanted him and kept closing its fist on his mind. Caleb summoned all the strength he had left to hold off its impervious grip.

The fisherman vainly continued his quest for shelter, but the rain and the disorienting motions of the boat made navigation impossible. The two men stood ten feet apart, but they could barely see one another. Sighting land was impossible. The waves pitched the boat high and then dropped it at incredible speeds, tossing the men like wheat in a winnowing fan. The storm seemed to penetrate deeply into the sea, as if God himself plunged his giant finger into its depths and stirred.

By pulling on ropes, fixtures, and whatever else he could grasp onto, the fisherman fought his way over to Caleb, who was holding onto the gunwale, nauseated and retching. "Don't worry!" he cried. "I've been through my share of squalls like this. It will soon pass. Just hold on. We'll be out of this soon."

Caleb nodded and tried to smile, but the expression he managed fell somewhere between dysentery and despondency.

Suddenly the boat jolted, spilling Caleb forward onto his knees, and he heard a horrible sound of wood cracking above the roaring din of the wind and the waves. He knew immediately that the boat had run aground, although they should not have been anywhere near shore. Caleb managed to get back onto his feet, but as soon as he regained his balance, the sea pulled the boat back from whatever they hit, and he stumbled, almost falling backward. Water rushed into the boat, and Caleb tried to ask the fisherman what they should do next, but before he was able to shout the question, the waves jerked them back toward the obstacle again, harder this time, and ejected Caleb and the fisherman out of the boat into the sea.

Water stung Caleb's eyes and filled his ears with a dull pressure. Unable to fight the instinct to gasp for air, he opened his mouth and sucked water instead of taking a breath. He fought frantically for the surface. Finally, he managed to burst out of the waves for a moment. He desperately wanted to gulp air, but because there was so much water in his lungs, all he could manage to do was make a strained, rattling sound before the waves pulled him under again.

Although he was underwater for only a few seconds, it was enough time for him to think a thousand thoughts. He thought of the lidless eyes staring at him from his bucket, calm and emotionless, alongside dismembered gills, tails, and other fish parts, not necessarily from the same fish. He thought about how weird it would be if his eyes rolled around in some old bucket with another man's arm, and the idea made him feel sorry for the fish he had ground up and swallowed. Those eyes in the bucket had once searched these waters. The gills had breathed the water that was now drowning him. Down under the water fish lived comfortably in a world made for them, while men who couldn't survive more than five minutes underwater hunted them from above, floating in the world above. Which world was real? Who could say water didn't matter more than land? At least it wasn't populated with the liars and manipulators who reigned the air and soil above. The truth was, both worlds were a part of something larger than themselves, a universe neither side fully embodied. They were merely parts of a whole, helping complete the real world. Water and air were both real, and they needed one another to survive.

Exhausted, Caleb kicked and thrashed, trying to regain his equilibrium, and finally surfaced. He looked vainly for the fisherman as he treaded water and tried to get his bearings. He had been thrown a distance of thirty yards, but he could still make out the battered boat, perched in a strange, lopsided position. The waves chopped at its broken hull, but it remained stationary. Part of it was underwater, but the bow pointed upwards, implicating the sky, and a good part of the deck aft of the mast was above water. Caleb guessed it must have gotten stuck on something.

The sight of the boat had distracted him for a moment, but his mind quickly returned to his predicament. He had never been a very good swimmer. Chilly depths enveloped him, and panic gripped his heart as he thought about his feet kicking eighty feet from the bottom of the sea. He fought the fear and swam furiously, reaching the boat just before he exhausted the little strength he had left. His fingers gripped the hull, and he rested, panting and hanging on for dear life. Suddenly he realized his feet were standing on the object that had pitched them into the sea and now suspended his boat halfway into the air. He could tell that it was a submerged rock structure rising from the sea floor to within a few feet from the water's surface. He had heard about these mysterious cone-shaped piles at the docks—ancient underwater cairns of unknown origins. Some said they were ancient fish nurseries, but others spoke of long forgotten, subaquatic tombs belonging to great kings, or earthquakes that pushed proud cities into the watery depths. Caleb had no idea what it was, but he was glad to have a foothold to weather the storm.

He saw no sign of the fisherman. What had become of him? Caleb worried, but he reminded himself that the fisherman was an excellent swimmer. He couldn't have been far away. For all Caleb knew, he was hanging onto the other side of the boat. He reminded himself that he wasn't thinking straight. The storm had bludgeoned his senses so badly, the fisherman could have been within an arm's breadth, and Caleb would not have known it.

He pondered the absurdity of his position. How did he end up in the middle of the sea, clinging to this awful wreck, standing tiptoe on a forgotten underwater pile of rocks? Why couldn't he be left alone? If he wasn't tossing and turning on his bed with night sweats and dreams, he was getting a beating from the priest in the public square or drowning in the middle of the sea! What did he do to deserve this?

"Why me?" he screamed. "Why do you haunt me in my sleep? Why ask me to question kings? Why do I have to scold the elders and the priests? Choose someone else. Let another poor sap suffer the bludgeons of your favor!" The wind howled in his ears. The sea sprayed and spat in his eyes, but he was seeing clearly. The seasickness helped clear his body of the poison he had been drinking. The fog had cleared, and he felt sober and light.

Minutes, maybe hours later—he didn't know how long—the storm rolled away. Caleb was surprised to see land within a few hundred feet from the wreckage. Having regained his strength, he took a wooden plank from the boat under his forearms and kicked his way toward the shore. He couldn't be sure what it was at first, but his eyes made out a long form stretched out on the sand. As he came closer, he recognized it was the fisherman lying on his back. He was still, and sometimes the waves lapped at his face.

Caleb reached shore and dropped to his knees next to the fisherman. He hovered over him, looking for signs of life. He could see that the fisherman had been bleeding badly from a cut on his right thigh, but he was still breathing.

He took the man's chin and moved his head left and right, carefully at first, then more aggressively when he didn't respond. "Wake up!" he cried, and he slapped him on the face.

The fisherman moaned.

"Wake up, you stubborn fool!" Caleb said, slapping him again.

The fisherman's heavy eyelids fluttered, but he struggled to open them. He kept moaning something Caleb supposed might have been the name of his wife.

"You've lost a lot of blood," said Caleb, stating the obvious because he didn't know what else to do.

The fisherman's eyes finally opened, and Caleb saw the consciousness return as his pupils narrowed.

"I didn't tell you," he said. "On the boat. I wanted to say..."

"Say what?" begged Caleb. "What did you want to say?"

"You never listen. Too hurt. Don't have the heart."

"I'm listening!" Caleb cried. He took the fisherman's hand and leaned in toward his face. "What is it?"

"Stop making yourself sick. Your burden. It's not a punishment. You've been chosen." The fisherman's chest flinched in an attempt to cough that ended in a pitiful clicking sound in the back of his throat. "Stop...stop eating guts and fish heads, and speak. The burden...it won't be lifted...till you speak."

Caleb watched the fisherman's eyes. The lids began to close. His throat ached when he looked at his friend, but he kept watching. He had a wife. Did he have kids? Caleb had no idea.

"Speak," said the fisherman. "Speak and be free."

The fisherman sucked in a final, broken breath and died.

Caleb followed the shore to the docks and found the bucket of fish parts on the wooden boards where the fisherman left it. He picked it up and tossed the vile contents into the sea.

He followed the well-worn path from the docks to the city. His clothes, what was left of them, were still wet. He sloshed along the way beside the city wall until he reached the gates and stopped. Between the gates he saw the priest standing in the courtyard, dressed in his clean, sacred garments. Caleb thought about his own tattered rags. What a contrast they made—the priest in his honorable robes and Caleb in his filthy tunic, damp with seawater and the blood of his friend.

Caleb took another step in the direction of his house and stopped again. He stared at the courtyard between the gates, the priest, and the platform on which the elders stood when they ruled against the farmer the day before. As he stood there, he felt the burden within him uncoil as it had on the boat the night before. Caleb no longer felt like fighting it. Maybe he had been wrong to drug it, to cage it within him and deny its freedom. Who deserved freedom more, the burden or the priest? Caleb realized that by imprisoning the truth he set the priest free to abuse the weak and manipulate the powerful.

Caleb entered the gates. The priest saw him approach and said, "Well, look who's here. The troublemaker."

"I may be trouble, priest, but I am not the one who is making it."

"I thought I told you to stay out," said the priest, studying the soggy, exhausted figure before him. "What's with you, anyway? Are you wet? Where have you been? What are you up to?"

Caleb ignored the priest and walked toward the platform within the gates. He felt the burden slowly wake and stretch from its long hibernation. He felt it loosen and then writhe within him.

"Go home, troublemaker. We don't need your meddling here. I have told you before. The king doesn't want you filling the people's heads with your delusions and dreams."

Caleb looked around and saw the priests and the elders preparing their dockets for another day of stealing houses and enslaving men, women, and children. He felt warm and light. Something rose inside him.

"Caleb? Need I remind you what happens to troublemakers around here? Has it been so long since your last beating that you've already forgotten?"

Caleb surveyed the courtyard and its surroundings. So many injustices had occurred here. He saw an old woman with a basket of fruit at her feet. She pleaded with her eyes to no one. He saw a dirty child, half clothed, running to a girl who was barely sixteen with a baby in her arms. The burden was slipping from his relaxing grasp.

Caleb stepped onto the platform.

"Caleb?"

"I saw a tower holding up the world," shouted Caleb.

"He was so light, like a sleeping lamb."

Delicate Hands

The door of the house burst open, and a chair's legs scraped the floor board by board, as though some hidden hand were pushing it, but it was only the wind playing its usual tricks, mastering invisibility and throwing rooms into disarray. The true cause of the disturbance was a real hand, more frightening than an apparition, attached to a muscular arm, and the arm was attached to a man matching the description of the arm.

A woman who had been sitting in the corner by the fire rose, startled. Before the intruder stormed in, she had been waiting alone in the single room of her tidy house, thinking it was the one place where she could feel safe. The man could not have known this because his sudden appearance startled her into motion, and now her body tensed into a posture very familiar in those parts, one signaling fear and an expectation of death.

"If you scream, I'll knock you down so hard you'll never make another sound," snarled the man.

The woman nodded, frozen somewhere between sitting and standing.

"Sit down. You're making me nervous."

The man closed the door hard, shaking the house, and came fully into the room, his bulk almost filling the walls with shadows. He doused the fire using a basin of water that had been sitting on a table, and in an action seeming too smooth and graceful for a man of his size, he pinched out the flames of all the woman's candles. The only light coming into the room now shone from the skull of the moon up above, most of which succumbed to limb and leaf before finding the windows of the house.

Staying low, the man peered out the front window.

"Say a word, and I'll kill you," he said.

Two miles away, a company of men followed a thin trail, barely traceable in the moonlight. Kihn, the one in charge, was tracking a big raider named Olin.

"It's faint through here," said Kihn. "Too well traveled, hard to pick out. We could be followin' my grandmother for all I know."

Because he survived the wars of Jehuda in the Megiddo plains, Kihn had gained a reputation for himself in those parts as a skilled fighter and an expert tracker. The citizens in town thought highly enough of him to appoint him town guardian. It was not as exciting as battle, but it had its moments. This manhunt, for example, was the kind of adventure Kihn lived for.

Shiah, the old merchant, had summoned Kihn after discovering Olin in his shop. It took some time to get the men together, and by the time they followed the trail out of town into the woods, he must have gained a good mile or two on them, but Kihn and his men rode horses, and their prey was on foot.

"It's too bad about the kid," said one of the men.

"Quiet. We can't think about that right now," said Kihn.

"I saw him."

"Shut up, Roan."

"I saw him layin' on his face. It wasn't natural. I never seen a kid that way."

"Shut up, will ya? Look! The trail leaves the road here."

The woman sat in the corner of the dark cabin, twisting a piece of cloth in her hand that, until a few minutes earlier, had been a garment for the child of a friend. She said nothing. She studied the hulking presence at her window. He seemed oblivious to her scrutiny, consumed by whatever was going on outside.

"My husband will be home soon."

The big man kept looking out the window. She could hear his heavy breath still trying to catch up from the exertion of distancing himself from an unknown pursuer. Soldiers? Wolves? Bandits? From the look of him she decided it had to be the authorities. He stole something or killed someone, and now he was in her house, holding her hostage.

His oily smell repulsed her. She watched him crouching low under the window, waiting as if he were in his own house. What made him think he could invade her home like this? It wasn't much, but it was tidy and in good repair. Then in comes this hairy oaf, nearly tearing the door off the hinges, infecting her space with his filthy giant body. The house wasn't much, but it was hers. He had no right to bring his trouble here.

Her anger overcame her fear, and she said, "Did you hear me? I said my husband is coming."

"I heard you," he croaked. "Why d'you think I'm staring out this window, crouching like a dog doin' his business, till my legs fall asleep? If your husband comes, I'll know about him before he knows about me." He stole a quick glance at her as he said this. It was dark, but she could make out an underbite in his jawline and large, round eyes. The eyes didn't pause long over her, but they made her uncomfortable.

"What do you mean to do with me?"

The man let out a bitter blast of air. "Lady, you're just something I tripped over on my way out."

"What's your name?" she asked.

"Olin," he replied with a grunt. He didn't ask her name.

The woman glanced across the room, looking for a distraction, any excuse to break the silence. She looked from the dishes neatly stacked on shelves by the table to the rug at her feet to the firewood piled next to the sizzling hearth to the empty bed in the corner. She scanned the big man who had invaded her home with her eyes and tried to penetrate the darkness to learn something that might help her survive.

Finally, she spotted a bloodstain on the sleeve covering his left forearm. “You’re hurt.”

“It’s nothing,” he said. “Banged it on something a while ago.”

She got up from her chair and rummaged around in a trunk at the foot of the bed.

“Go back to your chair,” Olin growled.

“That cut needs to be dressed.”

“I’ll worry about that. Get out of that trunk and sit back down.”

“I have some clean strips of cloth in here somewhere. It would be easier to find them if you hadn’t put out the candles.” Her back was turned to Olin as she felt through the trunk. Good or bad, a man was hurt, and it was her duty to tend to him. Besides, maybe she could get a closer look at him while dressing his wounds.

Olin left the window and grabbed her, pulling her up roughly by the arm.

“Let go of me!” she screamed. Olin’s hand covered her mouth to muffle the shouting. His rough index finger blocked her nostrils and wrapped around her upper lip while the last two fingers cradled her chin. He smelled like something unpleasant she couldn’t quite place, and she couldn’t figure out why he smelled that way. He dragged her back to her chair with the ease of a child swinging a doll by the arm while the woman kicked and beat him with her fists. His body felt like a sack of flour, and the blows smarted when she hit him, but she kept pounding. Olin shoved her roughly back into her assigned seat, still gripping her mouth with his huge mitt. She was starting to suffocate.

“I’m going to remove my hand from your mouth,” he rasped, “but if you scream, I’ll cover it up again, and this time I won’t let up till you quit breathing.” She nodded as convincingly as she could.

Olin let her go. She gulped air but kept quiet. He went to the trunk and began tossing things out, using only his good hand. He hurt worse than he let on. Olin found some rags and wrapped the wound over the shirt and went back to his post at the window.

After a few minutes of silence, the woman spoke. "Your best chance is to turn yourself in." She rubbed her shoulder above the arm Olin used to jerk her back into her chair. "Do whatever you want with me. You will not get away. The man who follows wickedness is followed by the Avenger. Everyone is followed by someone. That's what my father always said."

"You and your high and mighty father keep your mouths shut."

"My father," the woman said as she mustered indignation, "is dead."

"One down, one to go," said Olin.

For a moment, the woman forgot the danger she was in and the strength that had swept her away from the trunk like a leaf in the wind. "How dare you disgrace the good name of my father! Take it back!" she said. "You have no right. No right. My father was good and true. You have no right."

She spoke to the enormous back at her window.

"My husband is coming. The Lord sees and repays. You'll get what's coming to you." She shook her head. Tears streamed down her cheeks, but her jaw was set in determination. "No right," she said.

The sound of another rider penetrated the darkness. Kihn reined in his horse, the others falling in behind him. They were close to Jalen's pass, the trail that cut through the woods from town. Had they been making a straight cut through the woods toward the barley fields, they would have taken the well-worn pass, but they left the main road a long time ago, following the raider's meandering flight.

The rider rushed past them, and they immediately fell in behind him. It was too dark to tell anything, just that whoever they followed was in a hurry. Kihn spurred his horse and pursued, the other men fast behind him. The unknown horseman rode like the devil was after him, and it was all they could do to keep up. Whoever it was, he was bent on his destination, oblivious to the company of men pursuing him. Kihn pushed his horse harder, trying to come even with the rider. The path was just wide enough for two riders to pass one another. Kihn was gaining on him, but his men were falling behind, disappearing into the darkness behind him. No matter. He would apprehend the rider, grab his reins, and within seconds of stopping him they'd catch up.

But he didn't have to force him to stop because when he came into the man's peripheral vision, the rider pulled hard on the reins, bringing his horse to a standstill in a cloud of dust. He stopped so abruptly, Kihn passed him by a few feet and had to double back to meet him. As he neared the other man, he could see his face in the moonlight and recognized him immediately.

"Levi? Is that you? What're you doin' out here in the middle of the night?"

Levi blinked sweat from his eyes. He was a twitchy sort of fellow, a loner who kept to himself in the woods with his wife. "I could ask you the same question," he said, looking suspiciously at the town guardian as the rest of his men caught up.

Levi's horse was breathing hard and foaming with sweat. Kihn surmised he had been riding hard for a long time.

"That horse looks like he's about to drop. You coming from town? Why did you wait so late to head home? You could have spent the night in town and headed back tomorrow."

"My wife, she doesn't like to be alone out there. It's just her out there on Jalen's barley fields. I set out for town this morning with a load of barley and promised to return before dark. Took longer than I expected."

Kihn eyed the sweating horse. Levi had almost run it to death, and blood ran from a cut on its left flank. Some men are so afraid of their wives. Kihn himself never married. A soldier didn't have time for family. Besides, he had grown accustomed to making his own decisions and liked it that way.

"We're tracking a big raider named Olin," Kihn told Levi. "He stole a bag of silver Shiah the merchant was keeping for Jalen in town. Killed some poor kid, a boy."

Levi turned white and swallowed. "God, help us! How awful! Whose boy was it? Someone I know?"

"Don't know," said Kihn, watching Levi.

"How do you know it was him? Olin, I think you said?"

"Shiah walked in and saw him holding the boy, limp as a rag. The monster threw him down and ran off. I got this posse together as fast as I could, but he still got a good head start on us. We should be closing in on him."

"My house is just ahead," said Levi. "You don't think he'd hurt my wife?"

"After what he did to that poor kid, anything's possible. We're wasting time. C'mon, we'd better check out your house. It's secluded, just your wife in there. That's where I'd hide out if I were him."

Olin's arm was throbbing. He caught it on the doorframe of Shiah's place after the old merchant walked in on him. He had thrown the boy down in a panic and tore his forearm on the doorframe trying to get out. He hadn't noticed it before, but now the pain was coming in waves. He wrapped the rags around it, and that helped a little, but he had not had time to dress it properly. Pain hammered the dirty, sweat-caked wound, and it felt like a family of rats had gnawed out rooms for themselves and taken up residence in the meat of his arm.

He hated he had brought the woman into this. What else could he have done? His pursuers were on horseback. He couldn't outrun them. By the time he reached the house his heart felt like it would explode. He hoped he'd come upon an abandoned shack, but no such luck.

The woman stared at him from the corner by the fireplace. He knew that look—a mixture of judgment, contempt, fear, and revulsion. It didn't matter. This would all be over soon. Olin always knew it would end this way. All his life he had been blamed for everything. "Look at that face," they would say. "Isn't it obvious he did it?"

When he was about ten, some boys stole a little girl's ragdoll. They hung it from the clothesline outside and set it on fire. There was no investigation. Nobody asked any questions. Everybody knew it was big Olin. His mother made him swallow the truth and apologize. The girl glared at him, hating him just like the woman hated him now. His father beat him with a cane rod until welts rose up on his flesh. He insisted he was innocent and begged them to believe him, but they ignored his protestations. He was too big and ugly to be innocent. He looked exactly the way a boy who burns little girls' dolls for fun should look. So they ostracized him, beat him, cursed him, and left him out. This was the constant cycle of his life, and it was happening again.

He knew it would end this way.

"What did you do?" The woman's voice interrupted the painful drumming in his arm. "Did you hurt someone? Did you kill somebody?"

"No, not that you would believe me."

"Why should I believe you? You break into my house, twist my arm out of its socket, and shout orders at me. And I tried to help you!"

"Help me? Sure."

"I tried to dress that wound, didn't I? But an evil man will shun kindness and abuse, knowing no difference."

"You want to help me, lady? Shut up."

"No! I won't shut up. You have no right. This is my house, and I will do as I please."

Olin laughed. "You are stubborn, I give you that, lady. Look at you sitting there, straight as Aaron's rod."

"And it's Rebekah. My name's *Rebekah*."

"Rebekah?"

"Yes?"

"Please shut up."

Olin looked out the window. They should have caught up to him by now. Something must have slowed them down.

"Where's your husband, anyway?" he asked. "You said he's coming. It'll be daylight in a few hours. Where is he?"

"He had to deliver a load of barley in town. He is one of the managers for Jalen, who owns the fields. He left with a cart early this morning."

"He should have made it back by now."

"Something held him up. Things happen. He'll be back any minute now, and you'll wish you had never found this house." She said this with a proud air, as if she were the queen of a palace and not a poor field manager's wife held hostage in her own one-room shack. "You'll be sorry. My husband will return with help, and they will punish you for what you did to me. He'll come. You'll see. He's smart and capable. He started from the bottom, with nothing, unlike a lot of other men. But things will get better. Just the other day he said, 'Bekah, things are going to change. We'll get out of this shack and out from under Jalen and start a new life.'"

"Good for him," said Olin.

"You never answered my question."

"What question was that?" asked Olin. Her talking annoyed him, but it kept his mind off the pain in his arm.

"What did you do?"

"Just so your story's straight with the others, I stole a bag of silver and bludgeoned a little boy to death with my bare hands."

The words caught her breath and her eyes widened in panic.

"I didn't do it."

"Why should I believe you?"

"Why shouldn't you?"

"Because … Well, it's obvious. That's why you're here. You're …"

"Because I'm ugly?" asked Olin, turning to look at her.

"No! Because you broke in here and are holding me hostage."

"Just shut up. Please."

"Look, give me one good reason to believe you," she argued. "You can't do that, can you? Just one reason for me to consider your innocence."

Olin slumped into the corner. His arm was killing him.

"This afternoon, I paid the merchant a visit. Sometimes he gives me work, moving heavy bundles and things like that. When I arrived, the door was half open, but no one seemed to be in. I thought maybe the old man forgot to lock up, or maybe he finally keeled over." Olin swallowed hard before continuing. "I went inside to take a look. The boy was on the floor, just laying there. I wasn't sure he was breathing, so I got down on my knees to take a closer look, but even on my knees I was too far away. I couldn't get close to him on my knees like that without laying on top of him, so I picked him up, held him. He was so light, like a sleeping lamb. His body was warm, but he wasn't breathing. Then I felt something wet on my arm, and I realized his head was bleeding. That was when I realized the floor was covered with blood. So much blood. He was such a little thing."

Olin stopped talking. He was fighting his emotions, struggling to go on.

"Before I had a chance to get help, they caught me holding the boy with him bleeding all over me like that. I knew they'd think I was the one who done it. Knew they'd blame me. I dropped him and ran. Dropped him in the dust like a sack of figs. I was so scared. Oh God, I'm so sorry. He was laying there on his face. Oh God! Forgive me, Lord! I'm so sorry."

Olin buried his face in his big hands and cried, heaving and sobbing in the dark corner of the room while Rebekah watched silently.

"I might as well turn myself in. I'll be stoned for sure. No one will believe me. No one has ever believed me."

After a few silent moments, Rebekah spoke: "The boy. Who was he?"

"How should I know? He looked like one of the field worker's kids—black hair, about ten. He had this tooth hangin off a leather strap around his neck."

Rebekah let out a gasp and clutched her chest in the same place where the tooth had hung from the boy's neck. "It was a wild ox's tooth," she said, staring past Olin. "My father had a collection of them he pulled out of a skull he found on a hunting expedition. After he died, I didn't know what to do with them. I had Levi drill holes through some of them and made necklaces for some of the boys, the ones who came around."

"You knew him?" Olin asked.

"I couldn't have children," she said. "The boys, they came to see me. I gave them things."

"You gotta believe me, Rebekah. I didn't kill that boy. I had no reason to."

Rebekah kept staring past Olin like she was somewhere else. Olin wondered if maybe she might believe him. But suddenly she said, "You stole the money, and that poor boy caught you. You thought you could kill him and get away with it."

"No, Rebekah."

"Thought you could take the easy way, instead of working for a living. If it wasn't you, who else?"

"I don't know. Look, I ran here emptyhanded. If I did it, wouldn't I have the money? Where's the money? Do I look like I've got silver on me?"

"You buried it somewhere. How should I know?"

Olin peered through the thinning veil of predawn light at Rebekah and shook his head. "I didn't do it," he said.

By the time Kihn and his men came to the house, they'd been tracking Olin half the night. The sky was beginning to gray, but the house sat quietly in the valley. It was cold and dark, and no one stirred.

Kihn directed the men to pull up 100 yards short of the house, so they could watch from the trees without being spotted.

"What do you think?" he asked Levi.

"I don't know. It looks quiet, but there's no smoke coming out of the chimney and no light from her fire. It's cold. She would have a fire."

"Maybe she's not home?"

"She's home. Where else would she be?"

"Call her."

"But what if he's in there? Won't we blow our cover?"

"Maybe we blow our cover. Maybe she's knocked out cold on the ground. Maybe she's asleep, and he's not even in there. I can't make the call on what to do next until I know what's going on in there. Call her."

Levi looked around at the other men. Everyone seemed to agree.

"Rebekah! Are you all right?"

No one answered. The men sat still listening to the steady hum of insects.

"Rebekah! I'm with some men out here. There's a raider on the loose, a man named Olin. We followed his trail to the house. Call back to me and let me know you're okay. What's going on in there?"

Inside, Olin gave Rebekah a look of resignation and started to get up.

"Wait!" she whispered. "Let's see what they want."

"What do you think they want?" Olin rasped. "They want my head on a spike, that's what they want, and we might as well give it to them."

"Just wait."

"I'm here," she called to the men outside. "Olin is with me."

"Rebekah!" Levi screamed, "Are you okay? Has he hurt you?"

"I'm okay!" she replied.

Forgetting how adamant Olin had been about staying in her chair, Rebekah made her way to the window, crawling over the big man to get a good view. Olin didn't even look at her now and stayed slumped in the corner. "Move over!" she said, "I want to get a better look!"

In the gray light of dawn, Rebekah could make out five riders. She recognized her husband and Kihn, the town guardian. Her husband had dismounted and was straining his eyes to see what was going on in the house. Something wasn't right. Rebekah studied her husband's exhausted horse. What was missing? She took a deep breath to calm her nerves and concentrated.

"What's happening?" asked Olin. "What do you see?"

"Shh! I'm trying to think."

Rebekah carefully scrutinized every detail outside her window. Kihn, his men, the horses, and her husband. Something was wrong.

Then it came to her.

She shouted, "Levi, where's the cart?"

"Cart?" he asked, "What cart?"

"The cart you use to take the barley into town for Jalen. You always bring it back with you."

Kihn looked at Levi and waited for an answer.

"I left it in town. What's going on in there? What's he doing to you? Are you safe?"

"He always brings back that cart," Rebekah said to herself. Olin was now watching her with interest. "Why would he leave it in town? He'd just have to waste a trip going back to get it. It doesn't add up."

"Rebekah! What's happening in there?" Levi called, a little less forcefully than before.

"Levi, what's gotten into you?" asked Kihn. "You're sweatin worse than that horse."

"Are we going to go in and get him, or what?" asked Levi. He was pacing back and forth like a caged bear, and he looked like he was about to grind his teeth to dust.

"I don't think that's a very good idea right now, Levi."

"Why not?"

"Because your wife is in there, and there is no telling what that big fella might do."

Rebekah, still watching out the window, spoke to Olin: "Listen to me very carefully. Here's what I want you to do. You go out that back door there. It's still dark enough that you might be able to get away."

"What?" Olin's tear-streaked face filled with childlike bewilderment.

Rebekah took his chin between her thumb and forefinger to focus his attention. Olin stared back at her with a confused expression, as if he didn't know how to react to the touch of someone's hand.

"I know you didn't hurt that child," she said. "They just think you killed him because you look mean. But you're not. You don't hurt people, they just hurt you."

"But a minute ago you said I killed him."

"I know you didn't because I know who did," she said. "Now, go while you still have a chance."

Olin ran out the back door, and Rebekah returned her attention to the men in front. The long night had exhausted their strength. They shifted their weight from one leg to the other, unable to stand still, while the horses snorted and stamped the ground. Kihn was questioning Levi, who seemed incapable of making eye contact. "Just why did you leave that cart in town?"

"Why does that matter?" screamed Levi. "There are more important things to consider right now!"

"Strange that we should bump into you like that in the middle of the night," Kihn said. "Without your cart."

"My wife is trapped in that house with a cold-blooded killer, and you're interrogating me about an old farm cart! I'll show you where it is tomorrow."

While Kihn distracted Levi with his interrogation, Rebekah, the former hostage, stormed out of the front door of the house, walking fast with long strides toward the inattentive men.

Levi was saying, "Right now my only concern is how we're going to get her out of there!"

"Well," Kihn said, looking towards the house, "I think you can take that burden off your mind." Levi and the rest of the men followed Kihn's eyes and saw, to their amazement, Rebekah walking toward them, alone.

"Where's Olin? How did you?" asked Levi.

Rebekah slapped her husband hard on the cheek. "Why didn't you bring that cart home, Levi? Why did you leave it in town? And why were you coming home so late?"

"Rebekah!" Levi protested, "You know sometimes it takes longer to deliver the barley. The line at the scales was longer than usual, and …"

"'Things are going to change,' you said. 'We're going to have a new life.' Just how were you planning to make a new life for us, Levi? How was it going to get better?"

"Bekah! You know how hard I've been working. How hard *we* have worked! I've been saving. That's what I meant. Soon I will have enough to buy a field of my own. That's all."

"You haven't saved anything! You spend every shekel we earn as soon as we get it!"

"Bekah!" Levi said as he held her shoulders. "You know how hard I work! I do it all for you. For *us*. I'm building us a better life."

"You killed that boy, Levi. I don't know why or how, but you killed him. You! I had a bad feeling when you didn't come home tonight. I told myself this was a righteous home, despite how poor we are. That the Lord will bless us one day. That I am your wife, and it is my duty to trust you. I told myself that you were an honest man. But you killed that boy. I don't know why. Maybe you waited outside Shiah's shop until he left, thinking nobody was in there, and that poor child caught you in the act of stealing. I don't know. *But you killed him!*" She beat Levi on the chest with both fists. "You're so afraid people might find out who you really are. They may not know, but I do! You're a *murderer*! I'm just glad my father died before he learned the truth!"

Levi's face hardened. He stared at his wife for a long time while the others waited for his response. Finally, he twisted his mouth to speak. "Your father was a cheap, common, field laborer who left us with nothing but hard work on someone else's dirt! All I ever hear is 'my father did this' and 'my father said that.' You talk as if he owned the town! He didn't own anything! He was nothing but a pitiful, borderline beggar. Don't you see? I'm working to build us a life where we stand on our own two feet without having to take orders from Jalen or anybody else. Can't you see, Rebekah? I do it all for us! A good life. That doesn't just happen. You don't just pray, 'God, give me food to eat,' and it appears on the table! Your father never understood that."

"Well, he wasn't a thief, and he wasn't a murderer, like you."

Levi shifted his gaze to Kihn for support, but Kihn seemed to be waiting to see how this was going to play out.

"Listen, I'm not a murderer. It was an accident, okay? I never meant him any harm. I overheard Jalen giving the boy instructions yesterday about taking silver to Shiah's for safekeeping until it could be delivered to some rich landowner so Jalen could purchase another one of his fields. What's he going to do with another field? I'm the one who has been breaking my back all these years. That money is rightfully mine. So I took it. I delivered the barley, hid the cart in town somewhere so that I could make a quick getaway if necessary, and waited until Shiah left the money alone in the shop. I had no idea the boy was still there! You have to believe me. When he saw me taking the silver, he surprised me, tried to stop me. I reacted, knocked him away, and he fell against the table and hit his head. I must have hit him too hard. I didn't mean to kill him. *You have to believe me!*"

As the sun broke the horizon, the dawn light revealed Levi's twisted face. Kihn's strong grip held his elbow, and the tops of the men's heads hung off their shoulders like wilted flowers.

"How do you like our new life now, Levi?" Rebekah asked as Kihn helped him onto his horse. Then the men led him back into town where he would await trial for the boy's murder.

Rebekah found the tent where Kihn said it was, behind the tanner's under a huge poplar tree. The tall grass around it swayed in the breeze, and a large, wooden chair sat by the opening in front. She carried a bag and a skin filled with water.

She found Olin inside, lying on his back on a quilt spread over the ground. The daylight gave her a chance to see him in detail. Even in repose he looked menacing. Black curls stuck to his forehead, and his swollen eyes stretched their lids to their limits. She thought about how those eyes shied away from her the night before. Was he hoping for some unspoken agreement, that if he did not look too long at her, maybe she wouldn't look at him?

Olin snored loudly. Rebekah had heard him from outside the tent. He did not stir when she entered, although she made as much noise as she could by opening the tent flap and rattling the skin and the basket, hoping to wake him with her movements. She knelt beside him, hesitated, and then dropped her hand lightly on his damp shoulder.

The bulging eyes pushed through their lids at her touch. He coughed and said, "It was your husband, wasn't it?"

"Yes," she said, "my husband."

"I never thanked you for believing me."

Rebekah said nothing. Instead, she opened her bag and pulled out some clean rags while humming a tune she remembered from childhood. She carefully unrolled the filthy dressing Olin had applied the night before and dabbed his forearm with water so that she could peel the shirt away from the wound. When she removed the crusty sleeve, his arm ran with fresh blood, and she poured the water over it and blotted it with one of the rags. Then she wrapped it with clean dressing. When she finished treating the wound, she held it gently in her delicate hands, her human hands, to see if the touch could cure the throbbing pain.

The only time he felt her presence was when he was under the terebinth tree.

Terebinths

Elhan planted a terebinth the day after his wife died, long ago enough for it now to have grown to twice his height. He nurtured it with water and dung, pruned back the dead limbs, and kept the ground around it clear of rivals competing for soil, sun, or water. In the spring it flowered with red and purple blossoms, and then pea-sized fruit pushed out the blooms until they fell and littered the grass below. By summer, lush green leaves bushed out of limbs that spread widely over the top of a grassy hill, providing shelter from the sun. The branches stretched out into the sky as if the tree were a priest interceding on behalf of his supplicants. To Elhan, they were a mother's arms, and he often ran to them when he sought a respite from the world.

His wife had loved terebinths. They reminded him of her. Although he buried her frail body in the family tomb alongside the rest of the dead, it was the tree he ran to when he couldn't stop thinking about her. Trees yield better memories than cold stones.

One summer, their son, Silas, slipped on a wet, mossy rock and cut his knee. He held him in his arms and whispered soothing words into his ear while the boy writhed painfully, screaming, "It hurts! Don't touch it! It hurts!" but the boy's mother hurried along the banks of the river and disappeared around the bend, leaving him wondering if, unable to bear listening to her son's cries, she had abandoned them for home. The boy's knee had begun to swell, the bleeding hadn't stopped, and he began to worry that he'd never be able to calm him down when she came running back to them with something pinkish and yellow in her hand. She squeezed it, and it produced a clear, thick fluid which she applied to her son's knee. She told him the pinkish yellow thing was a gall from a terebinth. When insects chew on their leaves, terebinths bleed and form misshapen pods that look like crooked little horns. They're like scabs, only they form on tree branches instead of little boys' knees. She told their son terebinths are special because their wounds heal the wounds of others. She always knew how to explain things.

The night she died, she said, "Only a part of me is leaving you, Elhan. The best part will always live in your heart." But Elhan's heart was too ruined and desolate to house anyone, especially her. Anyone foolish enough to seek shelter within its leaky, bruised chambers was soon evicted by its two permanent lodgers, Bitterness and Regret. They claimed sole occupancy. What could he do about it? Nobody has much control over his own heart.

She had not come to live in his heart as she had promised. The only time he felt her presence was when he was under the terebinth tree. When it was a mere sapling, he visited every day. By the time it grew to match his own height, he visited less frequently, maybe once or twice a week. For a while he lost himself in his work, going there only on the anniversaries marking her birth, their wedding, and her death, and on the occasional Sabbath. But now he was there every day again, and he spent more time on his knees under its wide canopy than at home or in the pasture with his flocks.

He considered that maybe she didn't live in his heart or with the tree or with God or anywhere else—that she was just gone. But he couldn't accept that. He knew she lived. She was somewhere.

Yet he knew she was dead.

He replayed that horrible night in his mind too many times to count. Her shivering-hot body boiling in his arms, the black hair sticking to her cheeks, her fierce brown eyes, still strong and locked onto his, and her parting words—"I can't stay, I can't stay." He was holding her when she took her last breath. He knew she was dead, but her passing had not kept him from feeling her presence, sensing that she was still somewhere alive. He rejected the terminality of death, its finality a myth, some made-up tale told around fires to scare children. No one just disappeared. The thought was too outrageous for him to bear. He couldn't accept it, which is why he spent so much time now under the tree.

Elhan heard his son approach, but he did not turn around. He was too absorbed in thought. He did not want to be disturbed. He did not want to talk to anyone.

"Father?" interrupted Silas.

He didn't respond. He knew it wouldn't work, knew Silas would keep trying to rouse him from his reverie, but he ignored him anyway, just to have those few seconds more away from others and the barren life they represented.

"Father!" This time Silas spoke more sharply.

"Yes, son?" he said without turning around.

"Are you all right?"

"I'm fine."

"You've been out here all day. Sara says you haven't eaten anything."

"I'm not hungry."

He kept his back to Silas, still facing the tree.

"Papa?"

"Yes, son?"

"When are you coming back to the house? You need to eat."

"In a little while."

The two men did not say anything for a while. Sheep grazed in the pasture nearby, and occasionally one would bleat, trying to get their attention, but neither man broke his focus. The older man kept his eyes on the tree, and the younger man kept staring at the back of his father. It was a perfect day, one of those sun-tinted, cloudless afternoons when the air was so clear you felt there was nowhere and no reason to hide. But even on a clear day, secrets hide in the darkness of the soul, where the light never shines unless someone forces its harsh rays into those inner, hidden crevices.

"What do you do out here anyway?" asked Silas.

Elhan knew Silas deserved an explanation. He turned stiffly on his knees to face him and saw his son's face, which was frustrated and worried.

"I talk to her," he said, "tell her all the things I used to say, and the things I wish I'd said. I tell her about you and Sara and the animals and what I've been doing with my days. I ask her for advice, ask her to forgive me."

Silas thought about this for a while. "Does it help?" he asked.

"Help what?"

"You know, help you. With the grief, your sadness."

Elhan sighed a long sigh. "Some, but it still hurts. I will never get over it."

"Then why spend so much time out here? It's not good for you to seclude yourself like this. You should surround yourself with people who love you. You should be back at the house with me and Sara."

"You wouldn't understand."

"Sitting under a tree all day is what I don't understand. You say it doesn't help with the grief, so why do you do it? I'm worried about you! Why do you sit out here?"

"It's like this," Elhan tried. "When I sit under this tree, it feels like she is with me. I talk to her, and she answers. She tells me where she is, what she's doing. I don't know how to explain it, but when I'm here, and only when I'm here, she feels alive to me."

"But she's not alive, Papa. She's gone."

Still on his knees, Elhan turned from Silas to face the trunk of the tree again. The movement looked defiant, childish.

"So you're going to stay here? How long?"

Elhan did not seem able to hear him.

"Papa? Will you eat? Papa!"

Finally Silas gave up and trudged down the grassy slope to the house.

Elhan watched the breeze bend the tall, sparse grass and traced each root's wooden finger with his eyes until it disappeared into secret places in the earth. He waited until he could feel her again. Sometimes it took a long time. He had learned to be patient. He waited and steadied his breath. The air touched his nostrils lightly as it entered, filled the cavity of his body, and exited through his mouth, drawing out every distraction, every thought, but her. Finally she returned. Her presence soothed him. A faint smile parted his lips. He felt she was asking him to do something. He felt it more strongly than he'd felt anything in a long time. Yes, it was her voice he heard under the tree. She was asking him to do something for her, and he aimed to do it.

He rose early the next morning and left the house before anyone else stirred. If they knew what he planned to do and why, they would try to stop him, so he moved quietly, hoping not to disturb them. His bag contained few provisions—a skin of water, no food, and a small dagger with a wooden hilt. He hoped he would not need the dagger, but he had to be prepared. He could not fail.

The ferry was supposed to be running, but he did not expect it to have many passengers at this hour. Good. The fewer people there, the less likely someone would get in his way. It was foggy, and the morning light was grey, and as he passed the sheep in the pasture, one of the animals lifted its head from grazing and gave him an accusing look. He ignored it and hurried in the direction of the river whose current moved in the same direction as his heart, which was moving according to the whispers of his wife.

He came to the river as the sun was beginning to break. The fog still curled heavily in the valley, and the man was relieved to find no one else waiting on the dock for the ferryman to arrive. He wore a cloak with a hood he had pulled down to obscure his face, hoping it would keep anyone from recognizing him.

Soon the old ferryman arrived. He stiffly bent over and lifted the passenger plank, then motioned for the man to board. He had light brown, cataracted eyes, almost gold, that nestled in his brow like almonds in their shells. He wore a simple, short-sleeved, brown tunic cinched at the waist with a leather belt. His arms were tan and muscular from years of rowing. Elhan tried to read his expression for signs of suspicion, but the ferryman's face was hard and indiscernible, betraying neither thought nor emotion. He nodded a greeting, dropped the fee into the ferryman's calloused hand, and seated himself in the stern, praying no one else would arrive in time for the first crossing. The morning air was still as the two men floated beside the dock, waiting to see if any other passengers would arrive.

Finally, the ferryman wordlessly untied the moorings, cast them onto the dock's wooden planks, and used one of his oars to push the boat into the river's current. He began mechanically rowing a straight, lateral line toward the other shore. He faced the man with his back to his destination but conducted his work as if he were alone, so accustomed to the constant interchange of passengers on his boat that he had ceased acknowledging their presence long ago. Elhan averted his gaze anyway and turned his head downstream, pretending to admire the river as it disappeared somewhere in the distant fog. He tried to calm his nerves and reminded himself why he was doing this.

When the boat reached the middle of the river, Elhan cautiously rose to his feet and took a tentative step toward the bow. The unexpected movement broke the ferryman's aimless stare, and Elhan heard his voice for the first time. It boomed loudly on the water, surprising him because it seemed so out of proportion to the small, wiry frame that produced it.

"Sit down!" he said.

Elhan ignored the command and took another tentative step in the ferryman's direction. The boat rocked side to side in a show of disapproval.

The ferryman stopped rowing. "What are you doing, you idiot?" he shouted. "You're going to tip the boat over. Sit down!" The ferryman pulled the oars into the boat and used one to jab at his passenger, who clumsily shifted to his right to avoid the oar, causing the boat to rock even more wildly. Elhan tried to dislodge the ferryman from his seated position by grabbing the oar and jerking it hard, but the water had made it slick, and it slipped from his grasp. The ferryman was angry now, and he continued shouting at his passenger in a vain effort to get him to sit down, while Elhan kept advancing. He was now too close for the long oar to be of any use, so the ferryman dropped his weapon and from his seated position, grabbed his passenger's cloak at the shoulders, jerking left and right, trying to force him overboard. The boat rocked wildly in the river. They were now several yards downstream from the ferry's original destination, drifting in the river's current.

Elhan knew he had to dislodge the ferryman from his seat somehow. Forgetting he was on an unsteady boat instead of solid ground, he seized him by his hard shoulders and tried vainly to push him over the side, but the force of this movement had a greater effect on the boat than its steersman, and it capsized, dumping both men into the river, still holding one another in a struggling embrace.

Elhan involuntarily released his grip on the ferryman when he hit the cold river. He swallowed a mouthful of water as he plunged into the current and felt the sandy bottom with his foot. The water was not very deep. He pushed his way back toward the surface to get air, and spinning around to look upstream, he saw the ferryman, who was the stronger swimmer, making his way back to the overturned boat. One of the oars floated next to him, divorced from its partner. Elhan snatched it up and bounced upstream, keeping his eyes focused on the ferryman, who had reached the boat and was now trying to right it in the water, but he was having a difficult time because the water was too deep for his foot to find purchase on the river's floor. Vainly, he pushed off the bottom, stretching his arms as far over the boat's hull as possible, trying to pull it over, but the boat was too big. He tried this several times, too distracted to notice Elhan sneaking up behind him with the oar in his hand. When he got within striking distance, Elhan swiveled back and then forward, using all the strength he could summon to his arms since he was unable to anchor himself. The oar swung clumsily a few inches from the ferryman's head. The ferryman felt the air from the near impact and turned from the boat to face his attacker. Elhan saw the man's eyes widen in horror as he swiveled back for another swing. He heaved the fattest part of the paddle at the crown of the ferryman's head, and this time he did not miss. The oar vibrated damply in his hands and produced a sickening thumping sound when it made contact, and the man slumped with a moan against the overturned hull of his boat, then drifted in the current, half-conscious, face-up. Elhan pushed the limp body away with the oar to put some space between himself and his victim.

The river was shallow enough now for him to stand up. He planted his feet and braced himself against the hull of the boat to stop it from drifting. Then he reached as far as he could around the hull and rocked the boat back and forth, throwing his entire weight into it, until he was finally able to right it. He scrambled over the side and fell exhausted onto the wet decking inside the hull. He lay there, drifting. He didn't know how long. He may have slept for a while. He wasn't sure. The whole morning felt like a dream. He did not concern himself with the passage of time or whether he had seriously injured the ferryman or with the consequences he'd face for assaulting him and stealing his boat. He focused on nothing but the orders his wife's voice had whispered in his ear. He lay still in the bottom of the boat and let the sun dry his clothes. From the shore the boat must have appeared to have been abandoned. He lay still and let it drift with him as a stowaway toward the next town, several miles downstream.

Elhan sat up, peered over the side of the boat, and saw that he was already approaching his destination. Here and there mud-brick structures appeared on the shoreline, at first sparsely, then closer together until finally he could see a cluster of docks on the riverbank and the settlement beyond. With the oar he had used to bludgeon the ferryman, he steered the boat over to one of the docks and berthed it. He climbed out of the boat and stood waiting for some sign that would tell him where to go next. He could not hear her voice anymore. He thought about what she told him under the terebinth.

Mother—she lives in Haladin. Find her. I have a message for her.

She and her mother never got along. Her father divorced her for reasons that were never explained to Elhan. He pried only once, cautiously testing his wife's willingness to open the one door she always kept locked from him, but she refused. If there was a key to that door, she swallowed it long before they met, and only someone she trusted more than Elhan would be able to coax it out of her. And she trusted no one more than Elhan. "If you love me," she said, "never ask me about my mother again. She's alive, but I have buried her, Elhan. I have my reasons. You will just have to trust me." He promised never to ask again and kept his word for the rest of her life.

Now she reached out to him from Sheol to send him to her mother with a message. Perhaps she always thought there was time. There's always time. Until there isn't.

He obeyed his wife's instructions, although he had not figured out how to locate his mother-in-law—he never met her; he didn't even know her name. What was he supposed to tell her? He hadn't received the message, only instructions to find her in Haladin. He had found Haladin. What now?

"Say, fella, can I help you with something?" A young, dark-skinned man with a string of fish slung over his shoulder interrupted his thoughts. He was sizing Elhan up. "You look like you're lost."

Elhan realized his clothes were still damp, despite his drying out in the sun. His bag dripped suspiciously onto the wooden planks below, and his beard and hair were matted from the tumultuous swim in the river. "I'm looking for a woman. An old woman. The days of her years would be about eighty-five now."

"Uh-huh." The man studied him while rubbing his chin. "Let me guess. You've got spirits."

Elhan's blood ran cold. He swallowed hard. "How did you know?"

"I've seen enough of your kind to recognize the look." The man with the fish sighed heavily and pointed toward the settlement. "Take a right at the end of the path. Look for the thatched-roof hut with the scarlet curtains."

He found the hut without any trouble. It was in a high-traffic area where merchants, fishermen, and farmers frequented the road to and from the river, not far from the docks. Scarlet curtains framed each side of an open doorway, just as the man with the fish said, and a strong aroma confronted him as he approached. There was no door. He stepped into a cool, dark anteroom. A breeze blew off the waterfront into the house and stirred a collection of mollusk shells and chicken bones hanging from strings in one of the windows. It must have been a waiting room. Three straw-bottomed chairs lined one of the mud walls. No one was around. He stood on the hard-packed dirt floor and studied the room, trying to decide where to look next. Before him hung another scarlet curtain across a doorway, and he realized the pungent smell was coming from the room behind it. Judging from his impression of the hut outside and the shallow dimensions of the anteroom where he stood, the largest portion of the dwelling lay inside, where some kind of incense was burning.

He was about to move the curtain aside to take a peek when a voice from within crackled at him like thorns burning in a campfire.

"You may position within. No waits."

He pulled back the curtain and inhaled a headful of smoke. The air was stuffy and hot. There were no windows, and the only light came from a few candles distributed throughout the room. In the dim light he could see that the smoke rose from a shallow basin on the floor to the left of an impossibly scrawny, leather-skinned old woman sitting on a cushion. Her thin, white hair strung down either side of a wide part that tracked the middle of her skull. The smoke made his head swim, and he suddenly felt very light. He checked his hands to see if they were still attached. He felt like he was floating. The sensation was strange, but at the same time he felt safe, like he was in the right place. A sense of wellbeing washed over him.

The old woman opened her mouth to speak, and colorful lights flashed from her sunken cheeks. A rope of thick saliva tethered her lips, and her tongue rolled, unbounded by the encumbrances of an upper or lower row of teeth. "Have you come to perception the dead, or have you come to perception your destiny?"

He caught a movement out of the corner of his eye. Something in the dark shadows on his left. The pink muzzle of a heifer emerged from the darkness and bobbed. Another joined it. The cows shifted forward, and the shadows retreated so that he could see their faces. They chewed their cuds and gazed at him through innocent eyes. Soon an entire herd of white-faced heifers emerged, more than the room should have been able to allow. Instead of questioning their presence, he smiled beneficently toward them.

"Sit yourself!" the woman ordered.

His head was floating. It felt like it had expanded three times its normal size. He tried to obey the woman's command, but his first attempt at sitting failed as the air in the room thickened and bounced him upward. He concentrated and tried again, this time lowering himself slowly and deliberately to the floor until he sat across from the woman, face to face. The smoke was even stronger nearer to the basin.

His words slurred. "I've come with a message. From your daughter."

"I've offspringed no child," said the woman. She gathered a handful of seeds from a bag next to her on the floor and tossed them onto the fire in the basin. The added fuel brought a sudden burst of flame, which died down quickly. The smoke increased. He could barely see the old woman now.

"Your daughter," he said, "My wife. She's dead."

"So it's the dead you've come to perception? Dark your eyes. You must unsight the eyes to unclose the grave."

His eyes closed almost involuntarily. Why had he come? He couldn't collect his thoughts. He was supposed to say something. "I'm supposed to tell you for her. She thought she had time, but she had to go. She had no time."

The old woman didn't seem to be paying attention. She chanted something under her breath while swaying her thin body to rhythms he could not hear.

"Why didn't you come to her? She didn't know where you went. But I found you." His eyes remained closed. A satisfied grin crept across his face. "She sent me to tell you—"

If the old woman heard him, he could not tell. She continued chanting in an unbroken trance.

He felt like he was floating. He knew he should say something, but he couldn't focus his thoughts long enough to remember why he had come.

Then he saw her. He beamed at her, but she looked worried. He started to tell her he found her mother, but she stopped him. She extended one of her small hands palm up toward him, and he saw her unsmiling, smooth face, the face he thought he'd never see again, her brow furrowed.

Elhan squinted his watery eyes. "Is it really you?"

The woman nodded. The face was familiar—the olive skin, lips like sea currents, and cheekbones like unfurled sails against the storm of her black hair were all assembled into the vision of his wife, but he could not read the alphabet of her features. They were jumbled up into an expression he had never seen before. She did not seem happy to see him. She appeared hurt, disappointed, confused.

"I heard you under your terebinth. I came just as you said. Your mother—"

Go back! The features pinched her face together, and a tear rolled down her cheek. She shook her hair, and he felt a breeze that carried the damp scent of rain. *You went your way, and I went mine. We cannot be together now, my love.*

"But what am I supposed to do? I can't just go back. You said you would not leave me."

The face softened. *We'll meet again. The one who forks the path can piece it together.*

The image faded. He cried out to her, but she vanished into smoke.

He turned to the old woman. "Where did she go? Bring her back!" he demanded.

"It is hard to submission the dead."

"You know what to do! Bring her back! What is this? Are you still holding onto old grievances? That's all in the past, can't you see? She's gone now. Doesn't that hurt you at all? We've lost her. And you never came back. Never said you were sorry. She's your daughter! How could you have let her go?"

The old woman stared at Elhan mutely with a puzzled expression.

"I know this—I'd do anything to bring her back. Anything! She's better than you ever were!"

The man's head rang like a bell, and he could not see through the smoke in the dark room, but he was sure he heard a new voice, a familiar one, coming from the anteroom on the other side of the curtain.

"Father!"

Light burst into the room, along with a burst of fresh air, and the old woman's eyes grew larger as she drew back in response to someone coming toward her from behind him. A hand gripped his shoulder and shook him.

"Father! What are you doing here?"

"Son? I— Your mother, she—"

The voice spoke to someone behind him. He heard coughing, then a second hand slipped under his arm and helped him to his feet.

"Do you think you can walk?" asked Silas.

Elhan nodded dreamily.

"He's trashed," said the other man.

Elhan no longer flew. He was being carried away before he had been able to complete his quest.

Sara watched Silas's father through the window of their house as he systematically planted the saplings in concentric circles around the large terebinth. "Do you think he's okay?" she asked. An earthenware pitcher tipped in her hand and dripped water as her attention focused on the spectacle outside. She was young and thin, her body holding onto the girlish frame of a woman who had not yet carried her first child. She had arranged her dark hair in a single braid that fell down between her shoulders and pulled tightly against her round scalp, giving her the appearance of a twitching starling perched on a tree branch.

"He's better. It took a week to get the henbane out of his system. He must have had a splitting headache."

"No, I mean is he going to hijack more ferries and consort with mediums?"

"What can I say? He's mixed up. Mother's death hit him hard."

"Si, it's been twelve years. It's not normal, him nursing those trees day and night. He's neglecting his work—neglecting you."

The son peered out at his father and watched him dig a new hole, drop a leafy sprig into the ground, and push the dirt around it so that it would stand in place.

He turned back to his wife. "Leave him alone," he said. "He had no separate life apart from her. He tried to cope with it when she died, tried to distract himself with work, thinking time would heal him, but it didn't get easier for him."

"What did the elders say? Will he be punished?"

Silas chuckled. "Well, that ferryman is pretty mad. But he got his boat back in one piece, and I explained everything to him, that Papa was out of his mind with grief. I think he'll cool off. Papa should be able to stay out of trouble as long as he never does anything like that again."

"Will he?"

"Let's hope the new trees will keep him busy."

Elhan measured for each sapling, dug a hole slowly and deliberately, buried the roots in the ground, and poured a generous helping of water from the spring onto each new terebinth before moving methodically onto the next spot. He was planting a grove of trees, with his wife's in the center. He would still visit her tree from time to time so that he could remember her. He would talk to her, although he knew now that he had been a fool to think she had been speaking back to him. She was somewhere, but she was no longer here. And he knew that his only chance of ever seeing her again was to move forward without her.

He stood and arched his back to relieve the soreness from his work. He was out of water again. He dusted off his hands, picked up the empty wooden bucket which lay on its side, and started downhill toward the spring. Halfway there he stopped and turned to gaze at the larger tree. It was in full bloom now, its blossoms accenting the green foliage in red. The saplings he had planted encircled it in several rows. He planned on adding a few more, and then he would be done. One day, no one would be able to see her tree. And some time after that, he thought with relief, everyone will have forgotten that he had highjacked a ferry and consulted a necromancer in the village downstream, looking for his dead wife's estranged mother. Someday, everyone now living will have vanished, and no one will remember who planted the terebinths. They will only see the trees planted in a pattern and know they have a hidden history. That is all.

He stared hard at the tall terebinth and sniffed. "I lost my head for a minute there, didn't I?" His words broke into an expression that lay somewhere between a chuckle and a cough.

The terebinth looked back at him silently, its branches waving a tangled dance in the breeze.

"I can't bring you back. I know that now. We have to move on, you to your place, and I to mine."

He smiled wistfully at the tree, but he knew this time there would be no whispered assurances, no messages from the dead.

"You never really believed you could live in my heart, did you? You were just trying to soften the blow. You couldn't bear to hurt me. But it wasn't your fault."

Elhan picked up the bucket to head back to the spring for more water.

"I've got a few things to do before my road forks again and joins with yours." He felt tired, and his joints ached. He looked at the bucket and noticed it quivering in his hand. “We have to be patient,” he said. “It won’t be long.”

The terebinth seemed to understand and swayed in the breeze as if it were waving a farewell. Elhan turned with his bucket in hand and walked downhill toward the stream.

“He was splayed out on the rock like a crow’s foot.”

The Helpless Man

Samuel sat at the foot of his little girl's bed, but his mind still hovered over the pit where the man lay dead in black, pooling blood.

"I found a caterpillar today," she was saying. "Caterpillars make a sack around themselves and live there for some days and then they bite a hole in the sack and then they crawl out of the hole, and when they crawl out, they are a butterfly."

The sun bathed the pit in white heat. Dark, liquid wings spread from the man's back. His eyes met Samuel's. They were black, mothlike.

"Papa?"

"Yes, I hear you, Ruthi. Where did you find the caterpillar?"

"At the simmering lake."

She meant "shimmering." Her older siblings had named the lake after they visited it one night when the soft light of the full moon played upon its rippling surface. Ever since then, they begged their father to bring them back after dark so they could see the "shimmering lake" again. He made excuses, saying it was too dangerous to visit the lake at night, but in truth he preferred to spend his evenings at the Tangled Net, so the children had to settle for the bright reflections of the sun during daytime visits.

"It's time for you to go to sleep now. You're going to wake up your brother and sister."

"Centipedes aren't caterpillars. I hate centipedes." The little girl shuddered. She changed the subject every time he mentioned sleep.

A cool breeze lifted the curtains hanging from the windows in the room, but Samuel was suffocating. The moonlight by which he had been able to distinguish his daughter's dark, springy curls was momentarily obscured by clouds. The iron scent of rain hung in the air. Another wind roared in Samuel's head, a sound of angry screams. He desperately wanted to escape, to leave the foot of his daughter's bed, and join his friends for a drink at the tavern, but she had imprisoned him with childish neediness.

"Are you afraid of centipedes?" she asked.

The thump of the stone splitting open the man's head throbbed in his ears. The witnesses, former business partners of the accused, had thrown the first stones. He picked up a stone, too, and joined the mob on the rim of the pit where the accused lay pleading for his life, praying to God for deliverance. It was an ugly thing, but it had to be done. This was the way of justice. The law.

"Papa?"

The room was dark and still, but in his mind a sky ranged, bleached white by the angry ball of the sun. He tried to look down into the pit, but the dust-caked, sweating bodies of the men in the mob blocked his view. They reeked of horses and rope. They were shoving him this way and that, and enraged cries filled his ears. Another voice whimpered up from the pit: *Please, nooooo!*

"Are you afraid, Papa?"

"Will you shut up and go to sleep?" Samuel exploded to his feet, fists clenched, his jaw set in fierce consternation. "It's the same thing every night with you, hanging over your bed and listening to nonsense about caterpillars!" He trembled with rage and glared at the little girl, who curled defensively under the ticking of her straw bed.

"Papa, you're scaring me!" Ruthi cried.

The other children stirred. Thomas began sobbing quietly. Sara, the oldest, sat up and looked at him with eyes that seemed as if they were trying to discern the name of the demon lurking deep within her father's soul.

Ruthi wailed unabashedly.

Samuel roared at her. "I said quiet!" A hand that belonged to him but which seemed to operate on its own covered the girl's mouth and pinned her head to the bed. The hand was large, and she could not breathe. Her breathless legs thrashed and kicked the ticking off the bed.

A furious curtain parted, and the children's mother flew into the room. She seized her husband's arm and tried to wrest it from her daughter's face. Samuel released his grip on the girl's mouth, grabbed the woman by her shoulders, and threw her against Thomas's bed, hard enough to send it scraping several feet across the floor.

Thomas toppled onto the floor and took his mother's face in his hands. "Mother! What'd he do to you?"

Samuel woke up to the nightmare spreading out before him in his children's room. The children wailed. His wife scowled at him.

"Mary! I—I was just trying— She wouldn't—"

Mary got up from the floor, hurried to Ruthi's bed, and gathered the sniffling little girl into her arms. She tried to soothe her by smoothing her hair and glared at her husband.

"Mary, listen—"

"Go! Get out before you kill one of us, too!"

She turned to the task of soothing her daughter. The other two children diverted their eyes away from their father, whose figure loomed black against the window. The moon dipped low into its frame, a quiet voyeur who heard the children's cries for help and stole over to their window to peek in.

"I need a drink," said Samuel, trying to regain his composure. With that, he thrust his way through the curtain, snatched his cloak off a peg on the wall, and burst out, slamming the door behind him, not daring to look back at the stern eyes of his home, glaring orange with firelight.

When Samuel arrived at the Tangled Net, Harim and Bebai were already two drinks ahead of him.

"You look like a man who needs a drink," said Harim. He threw one of his fat hands up to signal the proprietor of the tavern to bring Samuel a beer.

Harim ran a local fishing business which had done well enough for him to hire workers to handle all the manual labor while he tended to the books. The reduced physical activity had swollen his girth until it challenged the poor seams in his tunic. He said he preferred to stay in his old clothes rather than buy new ones because the discomfort he suffered in his tight garments reminded him to practice self-control at mealtimes. If that was true, he never heeded these reminders. Even now, a plate of chicken bones pointed at him accusingly on the table. His coarse red beard shined from the grease of the meal he had just consumed.

Samuel dropped heavily into an empty chair beside his friends and stared silently at the empty space above their heads. The tavern owner dropped a tankard before him. He lifted it to his lips and drained it by half before setting it down on the table more loudly than he had intended, splashing beer so that it glided down the sides. Bebai, the quieter of the two friends, shifted his eyes toward Harim, and a grin invaded the right side of his cleanshaven face, the kind a man makes when he feels uncomfortable but wants to give the impression he has everything under control. His hands were light and delicate, as if they had been framed by the thin bones piled on Harim's plate.

"Were you at the stoning?" Harim asked, twisting his round nose in one of his hands to stop it from itching.

Samuel stared at the table. "Not only was I there, I helped."

Bebai adjusted his position in his chair. "You mean you—"

Samuel nodded. "I threw a stone," he said. He didn't add that he purposely missed the man because he was afraid to kill, or that he ran from the pit to a secluded spot behind someone's barn following the execution to retch without being seen. The other two men had found convenient excuses to avoid the execution that day and did not question him further, although he knew they doubted he could really hurl stones at a defenseless man in a pit, regardless of the crime.

"I heard the charges. It was necessary," said Harim dismissively. He leaned back in his chair and laced his hands together across his round belly.

"The witnesses were former business partners," said Samuel.

"Then they would know," Harim said, nodding.

"Or they had a reason to do him in."

"What're you saying?" Bebai asked, raising his black eyebrows, "that he was innocent?"

Samuel stared silently for a moment at a ring of beer that had run down the side of his tankard and circled its base. He sighed. "Don't pay me any mind," he said finally.

The door of the tavern burst open, admitting an old man who was clutching his left shoulder and breathing heavily. It had begun to rain, and he wore an old camel hide that was so soaked it dripped onto the floor. He collapsed into the empty chair next to Samuel and the others, probably because he was looking for a warm place to dry out and they were sitting at their usual table, closest to the fire.

The three men looked at each other and then at the old man, who did not yet seem to notice their presence. He sat quietly for a moment, trying to catch his breath, and then he tried to speak, but he fell into a terrible fit of coughing, lasting two or three minutes. Samuel thought he might be witnessing death for the second time that day. The old man hacked away, tears streaming from his eyes. It sounded like somebody beating tin with a hammer. Harim called for some broth, and somebody brought the man a dry blanket. After he drank the broth and warmed up, he calmed down a little.

"Much obliged," he said, "As you can see, I barely made it to this chair. I'm more ghost than man. Another mile in that rain, and my flame might've completely flickered out." He smiled like almost dying alone in the elements was supposed to be funny, his tongue peeking out of the broken windows of his grin.

"What were you doing out on a night like this, old man?" asked Bebai, who had a soft spot for old buzzards who are out on their own.

"I was part of an envoy of three men," he said, "now I'm alone." The air required for this last word triggered another coughing fit, which, the men were sure, was going to be the end of him, but more broth and some slaps on the back brought the old man's indecisive ghost back for another run at life.

The old man made another attempt at explaining his situation. "Conquest looms large in these parts," he said, "threatening the existence of this beloved land of ours. You simple farmers won't understand these things. No, you enjoy the luxury of scratching around in the soil, planting seed, and watching things grow while you exist in blissful ignorance, not knowing how close we are to the brink of extinction. I say this not to discredit you, my good men, not at all. The Lord prefers us to lead quiet lives, raising our families in charming pockets of idyllic tranquility. I'd say this world would be a better place if all men were such as you.

"But, alas, the Tempter whispers to men fashioned out of stronger clay, the kind used for modeling kings. These men are made for establishing justice and bringing peace into the lands over which the Lord has appointed them, but the Tempter, stooped and padding about on his toes, turns them to conquest. Yes, he sniffs these grander mortals out and lures them with visions of greatness. He promises them they can rule the world, and few can resist his charms.

"I sit before you half-dead because those who are supposed to be the strongest and noblest among men are, in fact, the weakest.

The Tempter has once again found another royal ear that will listen to his lies, and we are on the brink of war. As I said, I was a part of an envoy. We were commissioned by the king to deliver letters bearing his seal to two other kings ruling neighboring nations with whom he desires to form a coalition in hopes of staving off a war he knows we are not prepared to fight. The letters, which are no longer in my possession, contained the typical diplomatic ephemera, useless machinations of the lower kings whom God patiently suffers to rule the earth.

"We were the king's three most trusted men—I, your humble servant, the king's bravest soldier, and the highest-ranking priest in his service. We left at the new moon and were supposed to have delivered the last letter days ago. But as is often the case, things did not go according to plan.

"Our orders required us to cross the plains and then climb the mountain range on our northern border, crossing the Sheba pass so we could make our way into Syria. With God's help, our first two days were relatively uneventful, and by the time we extinguished our second campfire, we were set to arrive at our first destination ahead of schedule. But on the third day, we encountered the strangest set of circumstances."

The hot broth and dry blanket had renewed the old man. He had stopped shivering, and his eyes began to flicker.

"It was the third day, as I said, and we had already reached the Sheba pass. When you are in high places like that, the world feels different—the air is thinner, it's quieter, and the light takes on a paler shade. It's hard to explain.

"We had dismounted our donkeys and were leading them, making the pass on foot, when we heard a cry of distress. A few more paces, and we discovered the source—a young man strapped to a large boulder. He was splayed out on the rock like a crow's foot. Someone had driven four spikes, two on either side of the top and bottom, into the boulder and attached leather straps to them for the purpose of binding this poor fellow to a rock and leaving him to die in the wilderness. He was in a bad way. His wrists and ankles chafed under the straps, and his body was drenched in sweat. His eyes looked too large for his head, and his cheeks sank into his face. Judging from his frame, he might have been a large man once, but his body had succumbed to the ravages of hunger and was thin, emaciated. And nobody around anywhere for miles to hear his cries. Had we not passed by, I am sure he would have died from starvation, if the jackals had not gotten him first. I have never seen anyone in so much trouble. I pitied him.

"My mind grappled for some reason to explain the sight before me. Who brought this man up here, and why? Whoever it was must have planned the scheme in advance. Otherwise, how do you explain the spikes and the leather straps secured to the rock? There could be no doubt this was a form of slow, torturous execution. What had this man done to deserve such a fate? Why didn't his enemies just kill him quickly to avoid the risk of someone passing through, as we did, and rescuing him? The three of us discussed it. No one could come up with a reasonable explanation."

Just then, a gaunt young man shuffled up to their table. He was smacking and swallowing repeatedly while staring at the old man.

The old man greeted him warmly.

"This is Pavel. Don't pay any attention to him," groaned Harim. "He's moonstruck, crazy as a dizzy goose." He gave Pavel a stern look. "Go on and bother somebody else, you nut!"

Pavel appeared to understand and shuffled away. The old man smiled as he watched him go.

He returned to his conversation with the three men. "Let me pose the question to you," he said. "What would you have done? How do you think that man came to be strapped to a rock all the way out there on Sheba pass where no one could help him?"

"Obviously, he fell in with the wrong crowd," said Samuel. "He must have been a part of a gang that was hiding out up there in the hills, and they turned on him and strapped him to the rock, leaving him for dead."

"That is similar to the story the man told us. He spoke with an unusual accent, similar to the people of the East who do not speak our tongue, and begged us to cut him free. He said he worked for merchants, delivering spices and rich fabrics from the East, and made long journeys requiring him to travel through the pass on his way to his destination. He usually hired a few guards to protect him, but this time he trusted the wrong men, and they turned on him, stole his goods, and strapped him down to the rock, leaving him for dead."

Samuel leaned back in his chair, crossing his arms, and smiled with satisfaction. "Just as I thought," he said. "So you cut him loose?"

"It wasn't that easy," said the old man, dismissing Samuel's proposal by waving a hand in the air. "We knew nothing about this man. He could have told us anything. How could we know we could believe him?"

Bebai tried a guess. "Maybe he was traveling alone, and he was embarrassed to tell you that he had tried something so foolish. Maybe he made up the part about the hired guards, and it was really bandits who surprised him on the way, stole his animal and his goods, and bound him so that he could not report them."

"I thought of that too," said the old man. "But there is an obvious flaw in all of these explanations. Why would robbers go to all that trouble to stretch a man across a rock like that and leave him for dead? It just doesn't make sense. Robbers hiding out are in too much of a hurry to make grand gestures. They would have cut his throat and moved on."

"So what happened?" asked Harim impatiently.

"Well, I couldn't bear leaving a man in that condition, so I started walking toward him, intending to set him free, but the soldier snatched my arm and drew me back. 'What are you doing?

We don't know anything about this man,' he said. 'Wouldn't it be prudent to think about what we are doing before cutting him loose? He has survived this long. What difference will a few more minutes make?' Of course, he was right."

The old man lifted another spoonful of broth to his lips. "The soldier, the priest, and I withdrew a few paces away, out of earshot from the man to deliberate over what to do. I maintained that we should have pity on him and set him free, but the soldier had another point of view. 'We are on an important mission,' he said, 'a mission that could mean life or death to thousands of men, women, and children. We are trying to prevent war. We cannot jeopardize that by getting mixed up in this fellow's affairs. The stakes are just too high! Look, I'd like to help him too. I'm not made of stone. I can see that he is suffering terribly, but we just don't know anything about him.'

"'But what harm is there in setting him free?' I asked.

"'Okay, let's say we set him free. Then what? We can't just go on our merry way. Even without being strapped to the rocks, he's too weak to hike down the mountain. He has no food or water. He'd die whether we cut him loose or not.'

"'We could give him some of our provisions and carry him someplace where he could recover,' I suggested.

"'And where's that?' asked the soldier. 'There is not a settlement within fifty miles of this pass. Besides that, we only have enough food and water for the three of us, unless you have been stashing provisions I don't know about. We can't afford to split our rations four ways. We'd all be dead before we completed our mission.'

"'But we can't leave him up there to die alone!' I insisted.

"The priest weighed in. 'Your sympathies are admirable,' he said, 'but you are asking the wrong question. You want to know what we should do to help that man. But the question we should be asking is why would God allow a man to be put in such a situation if he were not evil to the core? The Lord is with the righteous and grants them good fortune, but his face turns against those who do evil. That man would not be in the predicament he is in if he did not deserve it. We did not strap him to that rock. His sins have chosen his fate. It's his own fault. We must not get distracted. We have a mission. Let us be on our way, lest we also fall into harm for ignoring the will of the Lord.'

"The soldier and the priest both made sense, but I simply could not get comfortable with the idea of leaving that poor man to starve to death or to be torn apart by jackals. Maybe they were right. Maybe I was being soft, and we needed to leave the man's fate to the hands of God, but I couldn't make peace with the idea without one last interview. I told the others I wanted to talk to him again and promised them I'd just ask him a few questions. They agreed to give me a little more time, but they had made up their minds and were ready to leave him behind."

A loud crash came from the kitchen, followed by obscenities. The men looked up and saw the tavern owner leading Pavel to the door, the shoulder of his tunic balled up in the fist of the owner's hand. "Go on and bother someone else!" he shouted. "I don't need you slobbering all over my kitchen." He shoved Pavel out into the rain.

The old man looked at the door after the tavern owner slammed it shut. "Where will he go?"

"Oh, don't worry about Pavel," Samuel said. "He can take care of himself. He lives in an old shack around the corner from me."

"Get back to your story, old timer," said Harim, irritated by the interruption.

The old man hesitated, then continued. "I walked slowly back up to the place where we encountered the man. I didn't know what to say to him. His story seemed plausible to me, but I needed something to convince the rest of my party to rescue him. Lost in thought, I came near to the place where I thought he had been strapped down, but no one was there! He was gone, and there was no sign of the leather straps or the spikes—just a bare rock! Had I forgotten where the man had been? No, I was sure it was the right place. It had been this large rock next to the well-worn path in the pass. There could be no mistaking it. I called for the man, but I heard nothing, just the thin wind of the high altitudes blowing in my ears.

"I ran back to my party and reported the man's disappearance. Of course, they did not believe me. Who would? Even I questioned whether I could believe my eyes. The three of us returned to the spot where the man had been, and everything was the way it had been before! There was the man strapped to the rock, helpless as a baby, in the same splayed-out position he had been in when we first encountered him.

"The soldier and the priest turned to me with looks of frustration, shook their heads, and muttered something to one another. The soldier drew close and furtively placed a dagger in my hand. 'If you want to show mercy,' he said, 'drive this into his heart and put him out of his misery. Or don't. But whatever you decide to do, do it quickly so we can return to our mission. Time is wasting.' With that, they joined their animals below the pass and prepared to depart, leaving me alone with the stranded man.

"I concealed the dagger beneath my cloak and stole nearer to the man, who didn't seem to be paying us any attention. He looked straight forward at nothing. He appeared to be half starved. I had a few figs in my satchel and held one out to him, then felt stupid when I realized his hands were bound. I could have fed him as I feed my donkey, holding the fruit to his lips, but the thought made me uncomfortable, so I awkwardly returned the figs to my satchel.

"Not sure what to say, I led with the question that wouldn't stop ringing in my mind. 'Where'd you go?' Maybe he'd think I was crazy. So what? Either he was stuck to that rock, meaning he'd never be able to accuse me of being a senile, hallucinating old man, or he wasn't, meaning I was right, and I had bigger problems than someone accusing me of being crazy.

"'What do you mean, where'd you go?' he said, 'I've been here the whole time, strapped to this rock.'

"'No, I came back, alone, and you weren't here. No straps, nothing. You had vanished. I know what I saw.'

"'Yeah, sure,' he sneered. He glowered at me with the most menacing look. It felt like he was staring into the most embarrassing secrets of my soul—all my regrets and shame—as if he could see things only God knew. I could have sworn he was fighting a smile. There's no telling how long he had been out there strapped to that rock, exposed to the wind and the hot sun, starving to death. I could count the ribs on his sides. He was a pitiful sight, a mere husk of a human being. He was the one strapped to a rock, and I was free. Yet despite his physical debilitation, an inexhaustible energy seemed to burn in his eyes. He may have been the prisoner, but I was the one who felt trapped.

"'Is it true what you told us? About hiring the guards who stole your goods and left you for dead?' I asked.

"'Every word,' he said.

"'Can you prove it?'

"'Prove it? I've got no proof beyond the predicament I'm in. I'm in the middle of nowhere, wearing nothing but a loincloth, strapped to a rock with no food or water. Why would I be in this situation if I had not been double-crossed? Look, I can tell there is a disagreement in your party over what to do with me. I know the soldier left you a dagger.' He looked directly at the folds in my robes where I hid the weapon. If he harbored any doubts, I confirmed his suspicions by inadvertently moving my hand to its hiding place. 'I saw him hand it to you. Do what you've got to do. There's no hope for me anyway. Just don't leave me stranded up here to starve to death. Nobody else will come by. Drive that dagger through my chest and be done with it. You'll be doing me a favor.'

"I have never taken another man's life. I didn't want to kill that man, nor did I want to abandon him in his time of need. But I could see the others' point as well. I didn't know this man. Who gets into situations like this? And what happened the first time I went back? Had I been hallucinating? I was beginning to think the whole thing was a bad dream.

"I drew closer to the man and pulled out the dagger, still unsure what I might do. The man looked right into my eyes, unafraid. 'Do it,' he said.

"I couldn't decide what to do. I had to stop the deliberations in my mind. I took a deep breath and tried to turn off my conscious thinking. The wind howled in my ears, and I fell into a trance, how long, I don't know. Then I snapped out of it. Having been momentarily abandoned by my mind, my hands had made the decision for me—I was already in the process of cutting the second strap away from the man's foot before I realized I was setting him free!

Harim broke in—"Was he grateful? What did the rest of your party think? Were they upset with you?"

"I haven't spoken with the rest of my party since."

"What?" asked Harim, stunned.

"No sooner had I cut the last strap from the man's wrist, than he grabbed me by the throat and thrust me against the rock, crushing my shoulder and rattling every bone in my body. I fell to the ground in a pile, unconscious. I don't know how long I was out. When I came to, he was gone."

"And the rest of your party?" Samuel asked.

"They were already dead when we reached the pass," he said.

A quiet feeling fell upon the table, and the old man stared at something in the fire.

"Then you were wrong to have set him free," said Bebai finally.

"I wouldn't say that," replied the old man. "I could go back to that pass a hundred times more, and I would choose to do the same thing again every time."

"But the man was evil!" Samuel said.

"All this time, and you thought I was telling you a story about a man strapped to a rock? This has nothing to do with him. His predicament and the circumstances that led to it do not matter. It doesn't matter whether he was telling the truth or whether he somehow staged that whole affair. Whether he was good or evil or an angel or a demon or the devil himself makes no difference. This story isn't about him. It's about the three men who encountered someone who appeared to be a helpless man on the pass."

"I don't understand," said Harim.

"Don't you see? There was nothing remarkable about that man or the way he was strapped to the rock. Each one of you has already collected your share of strange dilemmas in the thin air of life's passes, and you will, no doubt, encounter many more. There is nothing remarkable about that. Everyone sees helpless men.

"The truly remarkable thing, the story that's slightly different every time, happens within those crossing the pass. Some turn hard like the soldier and the priest and never make it through. Others choose mercy."

The three friends didn't know what to make of this. Bebai remained silent and listened thoughtfully, while Harim and Samuel argued with him.

"Surely you're not saying you made the right decision!" said Samuel. "You took a very foolish risk that could have gotten you killed and one that cost you the lives of your companions."

"As I said," the old man replied cryptically, "they were dead already. As for mercy, you are correct. Love is not sensible or safe, but that doesn't mean it isn't right. Mercy receives its rewards without seeking them."

The old man had just finished saying this when the door of the tavern burst open, and two men stormed into the room, soaked from the rain that was still falling in sheets. The taller man wore a sword strapped to his hip. The rain streamed down his powerful shoulders like waterfalls cascading down cliffs, but if he was cold or uncomfortable, he didn't show it. He surveyed the room quickly with a trained eye, as if he had done this a thousand times before. The other was shorter, and the rain made him look small, like a dog after it swims in a river. His fancy robes were soiled and wet, but he looked too angry and self-righteous for the cold to have bothered him.

"You traitorous pile of cow's dung," said the tall one. He was mad as a hornet. "We've been looking all over for you," he said. He was looking at the old man.

"Here I am, all in one piece," said the old man, and with great effort, he rose from the table, his body creaking like someone pulling open a rusty trap. "Thank you for the broth and the company," he said to the others. "Peace be with you." He walked past the men and through the door while their glares followed him out into the rain. The soldier and the priest gave each other a look of bewilderment mixed with rage and then exited the room as well.

It was midnight before Samuel started home. "Midnight." Such a misleading word, suggesting half the night was gone. There were still six hours until the sun exposed the world and its deeds again. Mary would still be up. She couldn't sleep when he lost his temper. He'd apologize, try to smooth things over. She always forgave him, but not before lecturing him about his drinking and temper.

When Samuel came within view of the house, he saw her standing roadside, waiting for him to round the bend. Was she angrier than usual? Did she intend on preventing him from entering the house? It had been worse this time. He was losing control, and he knew it.

"It's about time you got home," Mary said when her husband approached. "I've been standing out here waiting for you in the dark. I didn't know what else to do!" She sobbed into a handkerchief that looked heavy and damp, as if she had been using it for hours. Samuel timidly put his hand on her back, testing to see whether touching her might produce a negative response. She didn't react to him at all. The moon was full, and she looked broken in the pale light. He had never seen her like this. Lately they shouted at one another, if they spoke at all.

"Mary, I never meant to—" He suddenly felt very ashamed. He wanted to say he was sorry, but words could not pay for what he had done. Anything he could think of to say sounded cheap and hollow, like another attempt to buy more time until the next outburst.

She turned toward him and buried her face in his chest. His arms instinctively wrapped around her small frame. Her face was hot and wet against him. This was not what he had expected. Something had happened—something bad.

"Mary," he said, pushing her away and bending lower to look into her eyes. She stepped backward but wouldn't lift her head. "Tell me what happened."

"They're gone."

"Who's gone?"

"The children!" she cried. "Who else?"

Her eyes tightened in accusation, her face white against the frame of her thick, black hair. The bridge of her nose, long and perfectly straight, tilted higher. Her hand hung by her side, choking the handkerchief and probably wishing it was wrapped around Samuel's neck.

Samuel ran into the house and flung back the curtain that hung in the doorway of the children's room to see for himself. He did not know why he did this. He knew they were gone when

Mary had said it. When you're at a loss for meaningful action, you do meaningless things to fill the time.

Out of the corner of his eye, he saw movement outside the window. Someone was out there watching. Samuel ran to the window and looked out just in time to see the shape of a man's body rounding the corner of the house. An intruder! He burst through the front door and ran around toward the back of the house. Mary tried to intercept him as he passed.

"Samuel? Why are you running?"

But there was no time to answer. He ignored her and squinted down the dark road. He could make out a figure running in a broken gait. Samuel raced after the man and caught up with him easily. When he reached him, he grasped him by the sleeve of his tunic. The action stopped the man he was chasing but also pulled his body into conflict with Samuel's feet, and the two of them tumbled to the ground and rolled until they stopped in a pile at the base of the trunk of a ancient puckered oak tree.

Samuel's ears rang, his head spun, and the nausea he felt the day before returned. Stiffly, he stood on his feet while his quarry moaned. He was pulling the man up by the collar when Mary caught up to them.

"Samuel! Who is it? Did he take our children?"

Samuel held the man to the tree with one arm. His body was light and wiry, like that of an adolescent boy. He wore a hooded cloak that concealed his face from the pale moonlight.

Mary was panting, still trying to catch her breath. "Samuel, who is it? Do you know him?"

Samuel kept the man pinned to the tree while he pulled back the hood to reveal the intruder's face.

It was Pavel, the moonstruck boy from the tavern.

Pavel smacked his lips and swallowed.

"Pavel? Why were you snooping around my house? Do you know something about the children?"

Pavel swayed weirdly against the oak and smacked his lips. He shook his head.

"Pavel," Mary said, her voice in a quaver, "what did you do with them? Please, please, tell me where my babies are. Please, Pavel, please!"

"I-I saw them running. C-c-came to help but I was t-too late."

"Too late? What're you talking about? Tell me what you've done with them, you imbecile, or I swear I'll beat the truth out of that scrambled head of yours." Samuel's grip tightened on the arm he had pinned to the tree.

"Honest! I-I don't know anything!"

A swift blow from Samuel's free hand crushed Pavel's slack face and spun it like a wheel on the axel of his neck. He took the punch without protest, as if he had grown accustomed to this sort of treatment.

Samuel struck him again in the same place, right below the cheek bone.

Pavel squinted through the pain to plead to Samuel with his pale blue eyes. "P-please. I would n-never hurt your children."

The next blow caught him on the chin. It was lighter than the first punches, but it may have carried more force because it came from the children's mother. The action caught Samuel by surprise. He looked over at his wife and saw that the compassion and human sympathy had drained from her eyes and had been replaced by pure hatred.

The beating was making Pavel even more disoriented than usual. He feebly clutched at Samuel's tunic, more out of an attempt to stay on his feet than to fight back.

"Mary, get his other arm."

Mary used both hands to pin his other arm down to the tree. It was a large old oak, but the trunk was still round enough to bend Pavel backwards. To Samuel, he looked a little like a butterfly pinned to a display in some child's insect collection. Samuel looked at Pavel who was bleeding from his lower lip and panting hard from fear and exhaustion. He didn't know what was wrong with him, nor could he understand why he had been looking through the children's window, but he also knew in his heart that Pavel was telling the truth.

"Let him go, Mary."

"Let him go? Are you crazy? He may know where our children are. What do you mean let him go?"

"I know it isn't sensible or safe, but that doesn't mean it isn't right. He doesn't know anything. Let him go."

Samuel dropped the limp arm he had been pinning to the tree and nodded to Mary, encouraging her to do the same. She frowned and released her grip. Pavel looked back and forth at his tormentors with the eyes of a child asking to be excused from the table, but Samuel and Mary stared at one another as if they had forgotten he was standing there. Finally, deciding he should leave before they changed their minds, he ran down the road in the direction of his shack until he disappeared into the darkness.

"What will we do now?" Mary asked.

"Mary, do you trust me?"

"No."

"Look, I have an idea where they might have gone," said Samuel. "Come with me."

Forty minutes later they stood breathless on the shore of the lake. The moon was high and full, and its alabaster light played upon the waves of the water's surface.

"The simmering lake," Samuel said, repeating Ruthi's mispronunciation. Mary nodded at him hopefully.

"Samuel, I don't see them anywhere."

"It's dark, and it's a big lake. Let's look around."

Samuel and Mary began systematically looking for the children, working their way around the lake, searching behind the surrounding scrub, tall water grass, and white boulders. Samuel secretly worried that his hunch may have been wrong and that the children had been abducted. How did he know Pavel wasn't involved? The lunatic could have them tied up somewhere in that rickety shack of his. He kept these thoughts from his wife, who, driven by motherly devotion, was leaving no stone unturned, searching for her children.

This might be his last chance. Samuel knew that he was really the one responsible for the children's disappearance. It was his rage that had abducted them. Their home was no longer safe for them because he had allowed hatred to find the chink in his heart and fill it with its black decay. He had almost lost everything, but if he could get one more chance, he knew he could make it right.

Suddenly Mary whispered, "I hear something!" and she stole toward a large clump of scrub where she had detected movement out of the corner of her eye. She made a signal with her hand for Samuel to wait. He understood and watched her creep toward the bushes.

When Mary made her way around to the other side of the scrub, she found her three children huddled together, shaking from fear. Only Thomas looked at her, but he did not seem to recognize her face.

"We ran away," he said. "It was a mistake. We thought we could be happy here, at the shimmering lake. I want my mother."

"Everything is going to be okay now," Mary said. "Mother's here."

The boy still did not seem to recognize her. The other children continued staring at the ground huddled up with their arms around her knees, fixed in a hypnosis of trauma.

Tears formed around Mary's eyes. They didn't seem to be fully there. "Mother's here, Thomas."

The sound of his own name awakened the boy from his stupor. He shook his sisters. "It's mother!" he said. "She's found us!"

The children emerged from the brush toward their mother with looks of relief on their faces, but their smiles dropped when they saw their father standing on the shore, the silvery waves of the shimmering lake lapping behind him.

Samuel could make out their faces in detail from the soft light of the moon, the same true light that shined from the sun during the daytime but shining at an angle and therefore bearable, tranquil, and free. He knew they would forgive him. They were children, after all, whose hearts had not yet been fired and beaten on the anvil of hatred and vengeance. He knew they would forgive him, and this weighed heavily on him as they ran to him one by one at their mother's bidding. It sat upon him with smothering pressure as he embraced them and kissed their innocent cheeks, salty with tears they should not have had to shed. Samuel scooped up Ruthi in his arms and led his wife and the rest of his children back home, walking more stiffly now, lumbering and loosed, freighted with mercy's rewards.

He glued the pieces of the staff together and took an old rag and wrapped it around the spliced wood.

The Worst of All Lies

Every month, Amos left the solitude of his farm for the jostle and trade of the market. Few distractions overcame his general lack of interest in other human beings, but the market had a powerful allure. The bartering cries and sour aromas under its colorful canopies beckoned him away from the safety of the fields and convinced him to drop his rake, bid farewell to the goats, and saddle his mare for a trip to town. His farm was isolated, nothing but crows and a few jackals for neighbors, unless you counted crazy old Silas, who lived in the hills. He ate carrion, and you couldn't understand half of the incoherent babble that drooled out his mouth. Not much company for a young farmer trying to get started in a new place. The market was about the only social interaction Amos ever enjoyed, so he looked forward to his monthly visits, even if they strained his natural aversion to human interaction.

After his parents died, Amos bought a rocky patch of farmland using his father's inheritance and occupied it with a penful of jumpy goats and a few rows of corn. The farm had been poorly managed by the previous tenant. The soil was terrible, and most of the fences needed repairing, but the place was his. He was owner, manager, plowman, harvester, goatherder, and carpenter. It was hard work, but he wouldn't have it any other way. He liked living alone. Given the choice between working with someone who had his own mind about how to do things and running his own life, he chose the latter, even if it meant having to work harder.

Even if he had a bum leg.

Amos walked with a bad limp because of an accident on his family's farm after both his parents died. It slowed him down, but he functioned well enough. His crooked gait did attract a lot of attention when he was in town, though, which was why he preferred to be alone most of the time. People didn't know it, but he could feel them staring, wondering about his stiff leg, even if they stole a quick glance. He used an explanation he kept handy just for such occasions: "It's from a farming accident," he would say. "When I was very young, a log dammed up our river and flooded valuable farmland. I mangled it helping my grandfather free it. We ran a rope through a tree for leverage and tied one end to the log, and I had the misfortune of holding the other end when the log broke free. It pulled me through the tree and ruined my leg. It's stiff, and it hurts to put weight on it, but otherwise I do pretty well."

Amos told this story so many times he could repeat it in his sleep. He used to ignore the looks and the questions, thinking that was the fastest way to take the focus off his leg, but evasion only sparked more curiosity. He told the story as quickly and with as little detail as possible, hoping it helped people move on, even if he couldn't. While he was on his farm he worked unnoticed, except for the occasional jackal and crazy old Silas, away from the pity and judgment. People act as if they're curious because they care, but really their interest is driven by the universal human need to find a tragedy bad enough to make them feel glad it didn't happen to them.

Most of the time Amos liked the solitude, but he got lonely sometimes, which is why he looked forward to days when he went to the market. He could eavesdrop on conversations and nod at strangers just enough to keep his need for human companionship alive, like a starving prisoner living off bread and rusty water.

Amos had just bought a cartload of alfalfa hay and leaned against one of the poles supporting the tents on the far side of the market, watching some boys load it onto his cart. He paid them a shekel each for their help and watched them race each other to the adjacent field, their long legs kicking the dust behind them as they ran. He patted the horse, checked the traces, cinched the bellyband, and set the brake on the cart. He fed the horse some of the alfalfa, told her he'd return soon, and limped into the market to look for something to eat.

He walked with an abnormal gait, taking one easy step with his right leg, followed by another, labored heave of his left leg, his arms joining in the effort with the same irregular rhythm. Although it had been suggested many times, Amos refused to use a cane. He wanted to be normal and walk unassisted like the other farmers his age, although by insisting on walking without an aid, his limp drew far more attention to himself than a cane. He weaved through the crowds in the market. From overhead, he must have looked like driftwood in a river, out of rhythm with the water, trying to follow the flow, but clumsily failing to keep up with the current.

On his way to the other side of the market, Amos heard the voices of a group of boisterous young men behind him and picked up his pace, but the voices did not disappear into the din of the market. If anything, they grew louder. The men seemed to be following him. He could feel their stares. *They're mocking me*, he thought. *Pests. Mealworms.* He stopped at a booth and pretended to examine a basket of figs, hoping they'd lose interest and move past him, but when he turned to go, he came face to face with one of them, apparently the king of the mealworms. He looked at Amos the way a lion watches its prey and smiled unnaturally.

"Can I help you?" Amos asked nervously.

"The figs here are adequate," the king of the mealworms said, "but I can show you another place that sells the best in this region."

"Thanks," said Amos, "but I really must be going."

"Hey, what happened to your leg?" king mealworm asked abruptly, feigning concern.

"Oh," said Amos, annoyed. "I hurt it in an accident." He didn't have time to tell the story.

"See those men over there?" He pointed. Amos saw three more mealworms watching him about thirty yards away. "I told them you hurt your leg climbing out of the window of a brothel."

"Why did you do that?" asked Amos, angry and shocked that anyone would do something so heartless. How does someone come up with an idea like that? Did he lie awake in his mealworm bed made of rotten wood, dreaming up schemes to destroy the reputations of hard-working, God-fearing citizens? Amos felt dejected. Limping around on a bad leg was hard enough. Why did he also have to play a sideshow freak for the amusement of others?

Instead of answering his question, the king rejoined his worm subjects, walking backwards, shrugging and smiling at Amos. The others looked at Amos and laughed contemptuously.

Amos stormed over to the four men. They braced for his approach, eager for the confrontation. "Whatever he told you is a lie!" he said. "I have never seen this man in my life, nor have I in all my years ever visited the establishment he accuses me of visiting!"

"That's not what we heard," said one of the worms, grinning maliciously.

"I hurt my leg in a farming accident. My grandfather and I were trying to dislodge a log that had dammed up the river, and I was pulled into a tree."

The men grinned at one another.

"Look," Amos said, "it doesn't matter. The point is, I didn't hurt it climbing out of a window! Who are you going to believe?" he shouted. "*Him*?"

Amos lost his temper at this point and gave his accuser a shove when he said this. The countenance of the king darkened, and he lunged at Amos and might have knocked him off his unsteady feet if it had not been for one of the mealworms who caught his king by the sleeve before he made contact.

Amos sensed he was in danger. He tried to walk back the tension and reason with them. "Forgive my outburst, please. Try to see this from my point of view. This man doesn't know me. I've never seen him before in my life! Why would you listen to him? I'm the one with the busted leg!"

"That's just it," said a short sweaty member of the group with stubble for a beard. "Why would you tell us the truth if you have something to hide?" He looked at the others as he said this to see if he had impressed them with this argument. They laughed and slapped him on the back in support.

The commotion was beginning to attract the attention of the marketgoers. Amos decided to change his strategy. It would be better to beat a hasty retreat than to allow himself to be consumed by a pack of mealworms for the entertainment of the gossip-hungry crowd in the market. "You know the truth!" he said as he turned to leave and stormed off in the direction of the tavern.

In the market, booths covered in red and blue canopies lined walkways with just enough clearance for customers to pass without brushing up against one another, an important feature in that area, where the hills were filled with hot-headed sheepherders. Young girls helped their mothers unpack dates, figs, olives, and pomegranates. They followed instructions with brown submissive eyes while their brothers chased each other in the field nearby. A woman selling dyed wool nodded politely as he passed, and a group of wives stood at a table looking at pottery, picking up each piece and setting it back down, unable to find a match to the perfect prototypes in their heads. The voices, the shoulders brushing against him, the activity, the smell of food and animals—it all restored something in Amos he lost while working all those hours on the farm.

The teasing he received from the bullies still bothered him. He kept going over what they said in his mind. They probably had not left the market yet, and he feared he might run into them again. Amos wished he could smash those stupid grins off their faces, shut them up, stop the hideous laughter. But he knew it was futile to dream of revenge. Revenge dreams of fairness, but nothing's fair.

Besides, those mealworms weren't the ones who took his leg. If it hadn't been for his grandfather, he'd be whole, and he wouldn't have to suffer the stares and the mockery. He was young when the accident occurred. His grandfather should have been looking out for him. His parents had died, and he had no one else who could protect him. Instead of taking care of him, his grandfather used him as a farmhand, putting him to work on projects far too dangerous for an inexperienced young boy. If his grandfather had not been such a cheapskate and hired farmworkers, he would not have gotten hurt. Life may have been hard for Amos now that he was on his own, but at least he no longer had to take orders from that old skinflint. Even with a bum leg, he was safer without him. This was all his fault, and Amos could never forgive him for robbing him of a good life so young, before he had even had a chance to begin.

Amos was lost in this miserable reverie when he came to an abrupt stop. He couldn't continue any farther through the market because a large crowd clogged the flow of traffic. The crowd that prevented his progress built itself around a single booth in the market, the way a hornet's nest gathers around a solitary limb on a tree.

Amos pushed his way toward the front so that he could see. A gaunt old man wearing a shaggy hide sat at a wooden table with his hands folded. The table held nothing but a bowl covered by a cloth to keep the flies away and a sign adorned by two words written in a nearly illegible scrawl. The sign read, GOOD BEEF.

"Come while supplies last!" the old man was saying. "Beef from Israel's finest cattle that graze the lush valleys of the Negeb! You'll never taste anything finer! Eat this meat, and you will gain the strength of ten meals. You will not have to eat for another three days! Scour the earth as they may, Elijah's ravens could never find a better meal! I know someone's hungry. Who will nourish their bodies with these fine vittles?"

A small group of young men pushed their friend toward the table. He approached warily and lifted the cloth that hid the contents of the bowl. He looked back at his companions and smiled. "Should I?" he asked.

"Should you?" asked the old man. "Why, you'd be crazy not to. No finer beef can be found in this valley. You may never come across quality food like this in your life again. Take my word for it, you're going to need your strength."

"What's that supposed to mean?" asked the young man.

"Generally speaking," said the old man, winking.

The young man threw down a shekel, reached into the bowl with his fingers, and fished out a piece of meat. It looked dry and grey. While his friends urged him to eat, he opened his mouth, placed the meat onto his tongue, and with tremendous effort, took a bite. He had to wiggle the meat back and forth to break off a piece. He chewed thoughtfully for a moment, and then a look of alarm darkened his expression. He stopped chewing and twisted his face, closing his eyes tightly and shaking his head violently. Some of the women in the crowd gasped, and the man's friends laughed hysterically, slapping each other on the back. Tears streamed down his cheeks, and he turned pale. Sick and embarrassed, he ran away from the crowd so that he could vomit in peace.

Abandoned by the source of their entertainment, the spectators dispersed into the market to finish their shopping. Amos stayed back and leaned on a pole, examining the old man, who went about his business as if he had not been surprised by his customer's reaction. Amos watched him remove the sign, wipe it with his sleeve, and write something else. When he returned the sign to its position, it read, GOOD VENISON, in the same crooked scrawl. The same bowl sat untouched on the table.

Amos chuckled to himself. What was that crazy old man up to? He found a stool in the shade and sat down and waited to see what would happen next.

After a few minutes, the old man renewed his pitch: "Try this fresh venison, killed just yesterday in the Negeb, from a herd of deer hydrated in the rushing waters of the Jordan, the same waters once piled high by the Lord himself! Nourished on the green grasses of the Promised Land! The nourishing meat before me comes from a majestic stag skillfully hunted by a man of the fields who supplies me with the freshest cuts available in all of Israel! Any man who eats this venison runs faster and leaps higher. Any woman grows younger—you can watch the lines on her face retreat, apologizing for having ever appeared. Grey hairs return to their glossy black condition. Who will try the first morsel?"

Another crowd formed. Amos recognized a few of the spectators from the first round, but several new potential customers gathered, curious about the strange old man with the mysterious age-defying venison. A broad-shouldered, ginger-bearded priest wearing a black tunic two sizes too small for him approached the table and tried to lift the cloth. The old man slapped his hand with a speed that seemed impossible for someone his age.

"Why did you do that?" asked the priest.

"Flies," answered the old man.

"I merely wanted to look at the meat you have for sale. How am I supposed to know if it's fit for consumption? I think it's only fair to let you know I have received complaints about this booth. I just spoke with a young man who claims he ate some beef that made him ill here."

"He must have me mistaken for someone else!" cried the old man. "Can't you read? The sign says good *venison*, not beef!"

Several of the people who had been around for the old man's earlier performance roared with laughter. The priest turned around angrily, intending on scolding them for mocking him, but the size of the crowd that had gathered surprised him so that he forgot what he was going to say.

He turned back to the old man. "Are you going to show me what you're selling or not?" he said, his voice rising with anger.

"I can't allow everyone to handle and breathe all over my cuisine. I have standards to uphold! Only actual customers get to see the food after they pay. That's the way it works in every restaurant I know."

"What restaurant? You have a bowl of meat on a table!" the priest screamed. His forehead bunched together as if it were working against his eyes to keep them from looking at the old man who was making him lose his temper.

"Venison," the old man said, correcting him. "It says so on the sign."

"I don't believe this!" shouted the priest.

Someone in the crowd shouted, "Are you buying or not? Either place your order or move aside so someone else can eat!" More laughter erupted from the crowd, and the old man grinned.

"You seem skeptical. Perhaps you would like to try a sample? It's no charge," the old man offered.

"Oh, this is absurd! I'm not hungry, I'm just following up on a report that you are selling spoiled meat."

"How could anyone accuse me of selling spoiled meat?" asked the old man putting a hand to his chest with the affectation of a man who has been insulted. "I have come a long way to bring this venison to a region that wouldn't have access to it otherwise."

"Come now! You're joking! Admit it," said the priest.

"Sir, I stand by my product," the old man said, rising from his chair to hold the priest in his gaze. "You are a man who has a great deal of pride," he said. "A man the people respect. Your wife and children obey your every command. You never take a misstep, do you?"

The priest faced the old man, entranced while the crowd silently listened.

"A priest must be perfect, mustn't he? Never a wrong step, never a wicked deed. He would never do anything like—take a bribe, would he?"

The priest, now mesmerized by the old man's words, didn't move. He stood flatfooted with his hands on the table, leaning awkwardly toward the old man with his rear end jutting out at the crowd.

"Now," said the old man as he slowly lifted the cloth from the bowl, "be a good little priest and eat your meat." He reached in the bowl and lifted a slice of the boiled grey flesh to the priest's waiting mouth, which meekly opened to accept it.

The moment the priest swallowed, the spell broke. Overcome with panic, he spun wildly clutching his throat as the crowd looked on with a mix of faces ranging from amusement to worry. He wheezed and coughed, stamping the ground, and his eyes bulged out of his head. The priest had a ruddy complexion to begin with, but now his face turned blood red, and he seemed to be fighting for breath.

"He's choking!" someone yelled, and a concerned bystander slapped him on the back, trying to dislodge the meat from his throat. A few others assisted the priest, and after several minutes of trying to hold him still while he thrashed about, coughing and wheezing, they helped him dislodge the murderous piece of meat he had swallowed and led him off somewhere to lie down.

The crowd no longer paid attention to the old man and his gourmet meat sale and dissipated into little groups that left the booth one by one, the way spilled water dries, gathering into droplets and then evaporating. Amos watched groups of two, three, or more converse about where they would go next, what they would do when they got there, and how they would go home together. Soon only he and the old man were left.

Amos approached the table as the old man gathered his things. The old man looked up at him and said, "A full day's work and not much to show for it, just this lonely shekel." He tossed the shekel in his hand before depositing it somewhere in the depths of the hide he wore for clothing. He whipped the cloth from the top of the bowl, and Amos saw the meat curled up in the bottom, sleeping like rats in a nest. The flies, who had been waiting for this moment, attacked the meat ferociously, like vultures on a fresh kill. The old man took the bowl and pitched the contents into the tall grass behind his tent.

"Why did you do that?" Amos asked.

"It's covered with flies."

"No, I mean why did you go to the expense and trouble of setting up a booth in the market to sell rancid meat?"

"Rancid meat? I'll have you know that I sell the finest cuts in this part of Israel!"

"Sure," said Amos as he followed the old man out of the market. He carried nothing but the bowl with the cloth he had used for a covering folded neatly and resting inside. They came to the old man's donkey, and the old man took out a handful of oats and fed it to her while stroking her nose.

"Susanna has been with me a long time, haven't you girl?" He smiled proudly and continued stroking the animal. "Yes, we've been through a lot together." He looked at Amos and said, "She's a little depressed today, I'm afraid. She lost her sister, Joanna." He patted the donkey's neck. "There, there, Susie, don't be sad. You'd be proud of Joanna. She did good work today."

Amos suddenly realized what this meant. "You don't mean—Joanna? She was in the bowl? But *why*?"

"It's like this, my son," the old man said as he mounted the donkey. "Some people lie to deceive. I lie to wake the sleeping masses. I tell the obvious lies." He could see that Amos failed to understand the distinction. "The truth is always there right in front of us. We just don't see it because we are focused on other things. So truth sometimes has to stand on its head to get our attention. Get it?"

"Sort of," said Amos. "Not really."

The old man now spoke to Amos the way he spoke to the priest, staring into him. His eyes no longer flickered as they did when he spoke about his donkeys. Now they hardened into two black onyx stones, like the joints of an ephod, with a Urim and Thummim of their own, judging him as misguided and incomplete. "Find your home, my son. Then you may heal."

"Nothing will heal this useless leg," Amos said looking away from the old man across the fields.

"I'm not talking about your leg," said the old man. He clucked softly to Susanna and rode away from the market as Amos stood watching him go.

Amos found his horse and cart full of alfalfa waiting for him. The sun hugged the horizon, and rose-colored light bathed the canopies of the market with warmth. Amos checked to make sure no one was looking before he mounted the horse and then, with his good foot in the stirrup, lunged upward, keeping one hand on the saddle and slinging his limp leg over the horse with the other. His fear of being seen struggling to mount his horse renewed his frustrations.

Find your home, the old man said, *then you may heal.* Amos thought about his words. What did they mean? Could that crazy old man really know something about him? The thought of returning home turned his stomach more, perhaps, than a bite of donkey meat. Still, something in the old man's words rang true. Amos pressed his lips together and stared in the direction of his farm. Then he turned the horse and cart toward Beth-hadan, the village where he was raised and the home of his last living relative, his grandfather.

Beth-hadan was three hours on horseback from the market, and even though it would be dark before he arrived, Amos promised himself he would not stop riding until he got there. He didn't know what he would say to his grandfather when he saw him. It had been a decade since he had been home. He had not returned since he stole one of the family's donkeys and rode away in the moonlight to find a new life for himself. Now he was returning as he had left, led by the moon under a hood of darkness.

Amos didn't know why, but he believed the old man's words held the key to his whole life. Of course, the old man could have been playing with him, just as he harassed the priest, but he wasn't going to spend the rest of his life wondering what might have been if he had taken the old man's advice. *I'm going back home to finally face that old misanthrope.* Amos imagined his grandfather's bent figure clawing at the dust with a rusty tool, grunting in that way of his, like a pig rooting for grubs. *He got off easy when I stole away. Now he will have to hear the truth I have bottled up for the last several years.* His heart beat with anticipation. *And he'll see that I've got on well without him.*

Everything was quiet when he pulled up to the homestead, which he expected at such a late hour. He rode to the barn first so that he could unhitch his horse and feed it some of the alfalfa hay. The horse whinnied gratefully when he removed the collar, straps, and bridle. He found an old burlap sack and brushed her down quickly. "Don't get too cozy, girl," he said. "I plan to be sleeping in my own bed by the time the sun rises." After he spoke, he realized the only ears in the barn besides his own belonged to his horse. He had not noticed how empty it was before because he had been so busy taking care of his animal. Where were his grandfather's donkeys? Where was the old plow horse? Had his disappearance been so hard on his grandfather that he had to sell some of the livestock? Was he still farming?

Amos walked to the goat pen expecting to be greeted by several flop-eared bawling nannies, but all was quiet, and the grass had grown tall in the pen. There was no sign of life anywhere for that matter. The farm looked abandoned.

The house was cold and neglected. No smoke rose from the chimney, no lamplight shone from within, and in the moonlight, Amos could see one of the shutters hanging on a broken hinge. An owl broke the silence with a forlorn cry.

A sickening thought occurred to him, and he limped to the hill where his parents were buried. He and his grandfather laid them to rest in a cave and covered the opening with a stone. He came to the white rock wall of the cave and read his parents' names chiseled by his own hand: LILITH AND ONAN. Someone, he knew not who, had added a third. He tried to read it, but his eyes failed him. He recognized the individual characters carved into the stone, but his mind refused to string them together into meaning. He could not decipher them.

Was it another name? Had someone else been laid to rest alongside his parents' bones?

The letters nestled deep in the cold stone. He stared at them until his eyes crossed. Finally, they formed a familiar word, a name: ELHANAN.

At first, the name did not register. All thought raced away from him except for the letters staring back at him. His head became stone, the letters etched upon his brow.

ELHANAN? What does it mean?

A cold realization washed over him, shocking him back into a state of awareness. *His grandfather.*

So he too had died on this accursed farm.

Amos fell to his knees and gaped at the rock, rechiseling the name with his eyes, searching for another interpretation, trying to make them mean something, anything, other than the name of the man he had come to Beth-hadan to confront.

He remembered the old man in the market. How could he have listened to that old fool? Why was he there? *How does this help, old man? You said go home, but nothing's here. What am I supposed to do now?*

Confronting his grandfather wouldn't have healed him anyway. Amos had already tried that. He blamed his grandfather for being careless, and his grandfather told him everything was his own fault. Did his grandfather love him? Was he there when Amos needed him most? Did he fill in for the mother and father, whose bones lay in the cold ground? No, instead he complained that Amos should have let go of a rope! Letting go was impossible, but even if he could have let go, he would have held on anyway. He would have jumped into that tree and broken his leg himself if he thought that might have impressed him.

His heart turned to tar as he descended the hill toward the empty house. He stepped onto the porch and tried the door. It swung open easily into a quiet forgotten room. His grandfather's room. *Back in the old skinflint's lair,* he thought. *What did he do here all alone during his final days? How did he occupy his time? Was he strategizing his next plan of attack, trying to figure out how to draw me back home, squeeze more life out of me, when he drew his last breath?*

Everything was covered by a patina of dust. In the moonlight Amos could make out a few of his grandfather's meager possessions. A plate, a bowl, and a goblet lidded with cobwebs on top of a roughhewn table set for one. A lonesome chair. A walking cane leaning in the corner. A crude pallet on the floor covered with moth-eaten blankets. Ashes in a cold fireplace. Shelves littered with various pieces of farming equipment. A wooden bucket.

Amos remembered lying on the pallet, screaming in pain, longing for his mother and then remembering she was dead. He remembered his grandfather's face, creased with worry but disfigured by a mouth speaking mismatched words: "Shh! It's not as bad as it looks. Just lay quiet, try to sleep. We'll patch you up, and in a few days you'll be as good as new." His grandfather had dabbed pointlessly with a rag at his busted leg. "Accidents happen," he said. "If you had just let go of the rope. We could have found some other way. If you had just let go...." For days, Amos tossed and turned with fever, his grandfather hovering over him whimpering, "Oh, what am I going to do?"

When it became clear that Amos would never fully recover and would walk with a limp the rest of his life, his grandfather complained, crying to no one in particular, "Why did this happen to me? How will I get it all done? How will I feed the animals? How will I till the fields? Who will help me now?"

Amos, for his part, did his best once he recovered. He adapted and learned how to do the work. He was slower but not useless. And where was his grandfather? Out by the dammed up river, whittling away at a stick and staring blankly into the water. Amos couldn't spend his youth feeling like a broken tool. So one night, he gave his grandfather what he wanted, and he disappeared.

Amos stood in the middle of the abandoned house. *What happens now that there will be no healing?* he wondered. *I'll go back to that rock quarry I call a farm and till the earth two rows at a time, one with the plowshare and the other with my dragging foot. I'll grow old alone with no one to talk to except for an old crazy hermit, unless I drown or fall off a cliff before my time because of this useless leg. The people in the market will keep staring, the mealworms will continue to make up stories about me. And I will be buried and forgotten on that hill beside my grandfather and my parents.* This last thought stung the most, not because he feared death, but because no matter how hard he pressed his imagination, he couldn't envision someone caring enough to give him a decent burial. *It will be weeks, maybe months, before anyone will discover I'm gone. I'll become food for the wild beasts, and they'll auction off the farm in the gates.*

A thudding sounded in his ears, and his face flushed. All the pity, mockery, laughter, staring, and blame—blame being the strongest—surged, and Amos bellowed shamefully. He turned the table over, smashing the dishes, and raked his arm across the shelves, spilling the farming equipment onto the floor. He kicked at the pallet where he once lay in agony without his mother to care for him. He took the cane and broke it in two over his good knee.

As he was about to chuck the broken cane, a marking caught his eye, two half-moons under storm clouds over a squiggly line representing water. He recognized it immediately as his grandfather's manner of marking dates. The storm clouds indicated the second month because it fell in the rainy season. The half-moons showed the phase of the moon when the date occurred. The number of the symbols indicated the number of years. *Two years, the second month.* He knew what that date meant. It was in the second month, two years after his parents died, that the accident occurred. He turned the staff in his hands. His grandfather had decorated it with beautiful designs. It must have taken him a long time. Some writing near the top of the staff caught his eye. Amos read the inscription and realized it was his name.

Exhausted, Amos crawled onto the pallet and slept, cradling the broken pieces of the staff his grandfather made for him. He dreamed he was limping down to the river on his grandfather's farm. The sky shone like a jewel, and the closer he came to the river, the stronger his leg felt. He reached the bank, and found the river dammed up, just as it had been before. A forest of logs crisscrossed at the jam, keeping the river from following its appointed course. He sat down and watched the deep water pool where it should have been flowing. A voice spoke. The old man he met at the market. He was eating flesh, but it wasn't the sickening grey meat he had peddled in the market. Amos could smell its savory aroma. The old man ate ravenously, pulling the meat off the bone with the few incisors he had left. He smiled a greasy smile and said, "Take hold of that log there." Amos hesitated. The old man assured him: "Stop fighting futile battles. Take the log in your hands, my son. It is neither for nor against you. Let it take you where it will." Amos reached for the log, a fallen tree that somehow fit his grasp. At his touch it broke free. The dam burst, and the pool melted into a fast flowing river. The water roared all around him and carried him downstream. He held tightly onto the log and felt a peace he had not known since before the accident. He felt whole again. He kicked at the water to test his leg. It was no longer lame but was as strong as his good leg. His body floated swiftly in the current. The logs were all around him, but he was not crushed. The water bathed his face, but he could still breath. He inhaled the rolling water deeply and let the river take him.

Then he woke up.

He was back in his grandfather's house. Daylight streamed through a window into the room. He felt something in his hands. The cane. He was still holding its two broken halves in his hand.

Amos stepped out onto the porch and stretched. He hobbled to the barn, fed his horse some of the alfalfa, and patted her gently while he reflected on the old man's schemes in the market, the discovery of his grandfather's death, the broken cane, and the bitter blame he had been nursing in his heart. He studied the cane as he turned the two pieces in his hand. "I'll return," he said to the mare.

Amos hiked down to the riverbank. No logs dammed up the river as in his dream. Instead, the water rolled freely along its course. *Blame is the worst of all lies,* he thought. *One feasts on blame his whole life and finds in the end that he has been chewing on mule meat.* He found some resin in one of the old, bleeding logs that lay along the bank and applied it to the break in his staff. He glued the pieces of the staff together and took an old rag and wrapped it around the spliced wood. Then he sat down on the bank, holding the healing staff tightly in his hand, and watched the water roll down.

Defeated, the cloaked figure dropped the pale hand, revealing a face so shocking it caused the king to trip over his own feet and fall to the ground as he backed away from it.

The Leper King

Joshabad the king scowled at the sun as it burned the Megiddo plains in a red glow. He leaned in his saddle and spat on the ground near where his horse was munching grass. The animal nickered a protest, swayed its head in the other direction, and continued grazing on a fresh patch of ground.

"Looks like another night in the plains," he said.

He was leading a caravan from Rabbah in Ammon, where he had collected his annual tribute of grain, wine, livestock, and produce. The king looked back at the camels, loaded with plunder, batting their long eyelashes in the wind. Behind them the donkeys pulled five cartloads of winter stores flanked by the soldiers on each side. Bringing up the rear were the scarcest of all commodities—human slaves. He had been away for two months, and as he came close to home, his patience wore thin.

Huri, his captain, sat alongside him. "It'll be another two days before we see the gates of Samaria, sir." He said this stiffly, in his detached way, looking straight forward with his chin tucked under an unchanging frown. Joshabad thought he always looked like a man who had just been punched in the face.

"All right. We had better set up camp before we can't see. It gets so dark out here you can't find your hand, even when it's in front of your face."

The captain dismounted and began shouting orders. The obedient line of camels, donkeys, soldiers, slaves, and dust immediately began forming itself into a well-organized camp set in neat rows of canvas tents. After so long on the trail, the king's men could set up camp in their sleep if they had to, and many times they did.

The next morning, they broke camp as quickly and mindlessly as they had set it up the night before and were on their way by daybreak. The caravan made good progress all morning, snaking its way through the grassy plains, until Huri returned from scouting the road ahead, reining in his horse in a choking cloud of dust.

"What's wrong with you, Huri?" the king wheezed, "You almost blinded me with this accursed dust!"

"My apologies, king, but I have some disappointing news."

"What is it now?"

"The fords are flooded. We'll have to go around them."

"How long will that take?"

"At least another day, my lord."

"Will this dreadful journey ever end?" the king whined. It had been his advisors' idea for him to travel to Rabbah and receive the tribute in person. They told him it had been fifteen years since any Israelite official higher in rank than a captain had visited the territory, and unless the king showed his face and made an impression on the people there, they might begin to entertain rebellious notions. By making a personal appearance, the king assured continued submission and an uninterrupted supply of Ammonite goods for Israel.

Joshabad wasn't used to this. His father had blessed him by vacating the throne during a time of peace and prosperity. Aside from a few local skirmishes, he had never been called away for long periods of time to fight battles. In his twenty-eight years, he had never been away from the comforts of his palace for more than a couple of weeks. Israel was powerful and prosperous. Who knew how long it would last? Everything could come crashing down tomorrow. A king might as well indulge every fantasy while he can. That was his philosophy, and besides this excursion to Rabbah, that was what he had been able to do.

The captain led the caravan slowly around the flooding fords, searching for a pass that allowed them access to the Samarian foothills on the other side of the river. As they cut a new path through the wilderness away from the trade routes, they became more aware of their surroundings. The terrain rolled gently ahead of them, a sign that they were leaving the plains. Little blackstarts hopped in and out of the acacia and scrub, unsure whether they could trust this strange sight, never having seen an Israelite caravan before. High in the sky above them, the sun spied their course, punishing them with brilliant heat, the only respite being the quick shadow of a buzzard or a passing puny cloud.

Almost two hours into their detour, the king made out the form of several tan-colored tents along the river's edge ahead of them. Surprised by their presence in such a desolate area, he spoke to his captain: "Why is this settlement here? I know of no nomadic tribes dwelling in this area."

"Nor I, king."

Squinting, the king tried to make out bodies moving about in the midst of the tents, but he could see only two or three shapeless, robed forms by the river. He could not tell if they were male or female, young or old.

"Could be sheepherders," guessed the captain.

"Where are the sheep? I see nothing but a few tents, a fire, some farming equipment, and a few bodies down by the river," said the king. "I'm going to get a closer look."

"Do you think that's a good idea?" asked the captain, guardedly.

"If there is a settlement this close to Samaria, I need to know about it," said the king. "It won't hurt to get a closer look." He dismounted and led his horse toward the first few tents, still seeing nobody besides the three individuals by the river.

"Keep moving." A gravelly voice came from the tent closest to the king. "Nothing for you to see here."

"Come out here," commanded the king. "I want to talk to you."

"That's not a good idea," said the man in the tent.

"This is the king of Israel who rules in Samaria. We noticed your camp as we passed by, looking for a place to ford the river. Come out and identify yourself. We know of no one who has settled in these parts. If you are honest Israelites, no harm will come to you. But if you are enemies, this tent and every dwelling in this camp will be burned with fire. You'll come out, one way or another."

The man in the tent was silent.

"Huri, light it up!"

While Huri left the king alone at the front of the caravan to get the fire, the flap of the tent suddenly burst open, producing an apparition in rags. The king could not make out its face because it was loosely covered by a rag held in place by a pale hand.

"Leave!" growled the man. "It's not safe, I tell you! Go!"

More out of a sense of duty than desire, the king persisted. "For the last time, show your face. I mean you no harm. If you refuse to identify yourself, what else shall I assume but that you are an enemy here to spy out the land?"

Defeated, the cloaked figure dropped the pale hand, revealing a face so shocking it caused the king to trip over his own feet and fall to the ground as he backed away from it. The two pleading eyes looked normal enough, but below the nose the man's skin became white and cracked. Blood and a runny discharge oozed from the cracks in his skin. The man's lower lip was three times the normal size, making it impossible for him to close his mouth fully. The king was still on the ground, looking up at the afflicted soul hovering over him. He could smell its wretched breath, and it was all he could do to hold down the contents of his stomach.

"You're...a leper!" he began in a whisper, which soon crescendoed into a shout. "It's a leper colony! Move out!" The king's entire entourage staggered in fear, including the slaves, who began praying to their gods. As for the leper, he merely covered his face, turned, and went back to his tent.

The king regained his composure and called for Huri, who was already running back to the front of the caravan to see what all the commotion was about. They left quickly, finding a place to cross a few miles up the river. In less than a day, they rejoined the trade route and made it to Samaria. They'd left the leper colony behind, but the king could not shake the feeling that a part of it had been smuggled onboard one of his carts, and a stowaway was sneaking into his palace.

Three days later he sat on his throne hearing the first of several hundred cases that had piled up in his absence. The throne was made from acacia overlaid in gold, and its arms had been carved into magnificent twin lions that flanked the king on either side, adding further to the air of authority. A farmer stood before him complaining about some land dispute while the lions stared menacingly. The king's hands caressed their rich manes, but his face was vacant, inscrutable. He could not focus on land disputes, petty religious squabbles, and violations of obscure kingdom ordinances right now. All he could think about was the leper's mouth hanging agape, the yellow, chipped teeth, the stale breath he could still smell, and the purple, fat bottom lip spilling drool on the ground. His body sat on the throne in his palace in Samaria, but his mind was still in the leper colony. He carried its poison air in his lungs. He knew he was doomed. He imagined himself sitting on his throne, petting just one of the lions because he had only one hand to rest on its head, the other arm ending abruptly in a white-scabbed nub. He winced at the thought of raw skin that turned even the finest silk into sackcloth, the awful white scales, the oozing sores…

"My king?"

The farmer waited for a response. All eyes focused on the king. He surveyed the room of inquiring faces and realized he could not go on like this. He had to settle the matter.

"We'll have to continue this hearing at another time. A more pressing issue grips me at the moment." He dismissed the farmer with a wave of the hand and barked an order to a puzzled advisor standing nearby. "Call the priest."

The priest entered moments later and bowed theatrically before the king. He wore linen covered with a golden ephod. A turban adorned his head, and sparkling rings choked the sausages he used for fingers. His narrow eyes watered continuously from poor health, giving the impression of great compassion to those who did not know him well. Never one to miss an opportunity for securing his position as the highest-ranking official in the kingdom, he had come down from the hill country of Ephraim to welcome the king home. "I trust the Lord protected you on your journey?" he asked.

"He did," replied the king. "Thanks in part to your continuous prayers." Joshabad couldn't stand the priest. He concentrated on holding the smile he had conjured up and got straight to the point.

"Did you know about the leper colony north of the trade routes along the river?"

The priest shrugged. "No, my king. That is a remote location. Nobody has much reason to go there, which makes it the perfect place for lepers, poor souls. How did you come to know about it?"

"No matter," said the king dismissively. "I have a request."

"Name it," said the priest. "I am ever the servant of my lord."

Joshabad had to work hard to keep his eyes from rolling.

"Uzzi, the blind prophet. Do you know him?"

"An onerous wretch, that one," said the priest shaking his head. "Trouble follows him wherever he goes!"

"I want you to find him and bring him to me."

The priest's disposition darkened. "Find him? Your majesty! I— If it's counsel that you need, the entire priesthood is at your service. Perhaps you would like to inquire of the Lord? Or maybe my lord has dreamed a dream and requires an interpretation. I assure you, there is no need—"

"Get Uzzi I said!" barked the king.

Any further protests were pointless. The heavy priest lowered his eyes, bowed, and exited the throne room.

The following morning the priest returned, followed by a lanky man in a plain brown tunic who struggled against the soldiers who were leading him, one on each arm, into the king's presence. Joshabad had heard his clear voice bouncing off the marble walls of the palace hallways before he had entered. "Let go of me, you beast!" he shouted.

The priest was sweating more than usual. "Uzzi, the seer of Beeroth," he said, as if the man needed an introduction.

"Let him go," ordered the king. He examined the prophet before him. His father had always shunned the man's guidance and warned him never to call upon him for counsel. He had a reputation for rubbing Israel's kings the wrong way. That may have been true, but it was also true that all the calamity he had predicted came to pass. Earthquakes, floods, stillborn babies, humiliating military losses, assassinations. It all came true.

His eyes were useless. They stared into the air somewhere above Joshabad, two cold gray orbs, and the king could not shake the feeling that they received some kind of light, albeit an unearthly illumination invisible to others.

"You already smell like one of them," sneered the prophet.

The words sent a jolt through the king. "Everyone out!" he ordered. "I want to be alone with the seer."

The priest issued a meek protest. "Sir, if I may be so bold—do you think that's a good idea? This man, he—"

"Out!" The king shouted so loudly his voice echoed throughout the palace precincts. Soldiers and advisors scrambled to get out of the room. A peacock had strutted behind the priest without his knowing it, and he almost tripped over it when he spun around to flee the room. Within seconds, the frenzy died, and the prophet and the king were alone. The room was dark and cool, and a ray of light beamed through a high window and crossed the prophet's sightless eyes.

"You have taken me from my home by force. I do not want to be here."

"Of course you may go! Take gold or grain or whatever you desire with you. But only after you do this one thing for me. It will be easy for you, hardly anything at all, but it will mean a great deal to me."

"You kings are all alike. Every time I'm brought here, I'm asked about the unknown—the outcome of some battle yet to be fought or the name of a spy in the court. And every time I reveal the answer, you act as though I am somehow responsible! As if I control destiny. You want to know what lies ahead, am I right?"

"Tell me what you know, seer. Do you not have enough respect for your king to reveal your secrets?"

Uzzi looked just to the right of the king's face, toward an empty space, as blind men often do. "Look within your heart. You already know the answer."

"How can you say that?" cried Joshabad. "I'm no prophet! It is you who has the gift of God to read men's hearts. You can see events before they happen, not I! You know how to interpret that which is bound in dark riddles, to unfurl the unknown like a scroll."

"I have no more control over what will be than you! I am no God!"

"No, but he whispers his secrets into your ears, the fates that he designs for the world of men."

"Oh is that how it works?" Uzzi laughed dryly. "You think God built all this? He placed you on your throne, eh? Made you his anointed." The last word dripped with sarcasm, and the blind man laughed harder this time, slapping his knee.

The mockery was starting to wear on Joshabad's patience. He was not accustomed to being the butt of anyone's jokes. "I am king in Israel," he shouted, "and I demand to know what you're not telling me! Speak, prophet, or you'll hang from the gallows!"

"Now, see what I mean? There you go controlling destiny."

"You know something, and by God I'll get it out of you."

Uzzi grew serious. "Forgive me for asking, your grace, but may I have a chair? They forced me to walk here from my home. I have been on my feet so long they are beginning to burn."

The king left his throne and pulled one of the cushioned chairs from a corner of the room over to Uzzi. Then he carefully guided the blind man into a seated position and made sure he was comfortable. In the company of his men, the action would have felt beneath him, but here, alone with the prophet, he felt like the lesser man. Despite all his bluster, he knew he needed Uzzi, and the prophet, who possessed the knowledge he desired, needed nothing more than to be left alone. He had truth, and so he was free.

"I'll try to explain," the prophet started, the fog in his eyes seeming to spin like a pair of hurricanes. "You have no future, only now. The future's just a myth we made up to convince ourselves we'll have more time. We say, 'I'll plow the thirty acres on the south side of the river tomorrow,' or, 'We can arrange for our son's apprenticeship next year,' or, 'Give him some time. He'll cool off, and we can deal with him later.' But if we ever get around to doing any of those things, they won't be done 'tomorrow' or 'next year' or 'later.' We can only plow fields, make educational arrangements, and smooth over relational conflicts now, in the present. You see?

"I knew a farmer who dreamed of building a beautiful house with a stone spiral staircase going up the middle. He drew plans and collected supplies for years, but he was an old man before he laid the first stone. Before then, he made excuses about being too busy with his crops or taking care of the animals. When his two sons grew old enough to take the load of the farm work off of him, he had no more excuses, so he started building the house. The spiral staircase was the first thing he built. He said because the staircase was supposed to be the highlight of the house, it should be built first, exactly the way he saw it in his imagination, and everything else should be adjusted around it. It took him two years to build it. I don't know how he did it. Somehow he built a freestanding, three-story spiral staircase without having to ruin its beauty with unsightly braces or supports, at least that is what I'm told. Ten men once stood on it to test its strength, and it held strong. He had built an architectural wonder. People kept asking him when he was going to build the rest of the house. He told them it had taken a lot of energy and resources to build the staircase and he needed to build up his strength for phase two. A year went by, and he was still putting it off. 'Next month,' he said. 'Next week.' 'Tomorrow.' But he never made it past the spiral staircase. He's been dead for twenty years now, but if you go out to his place, you can see that beautiful stone monument to a nonexistent future, screwing up toward the sky.

"So let's dispense with talk of the future, as if it's something that has already happened, or some land you're visiting like a Phoenician crossing the Great Sea on his ship. There is no future. Yet."

"But you know things," said the king.

"Yes, I know things, things no one knows but God. But that is not exactly true, is it? Every secret I know is known by three: myself, God, and one other man."

"There is another?"

"Oh yes, always."

"Who is he?" The king's anger was rising again. "If you refuse to speak of my destiny, maybe he will!"

The blind man hung his head and thought for a moment. "You can see," he said, "and yet you are so blind."

"I can see well enough to know you're toying with me! Perhaps you will have a change of heart after I have someone stripe your back!"

"You are the third man!" Uzzi roared. "Three men know your destiny! I, God, and you, king!"

The king stumbled backward and dropped into his throne, stunned by the prophet's words. "What do you mean? Does some latent power lie within me to divine my own future?"

"There is no *future*. This is what I've been trying to tell you."

"How, then, do you predict what doesn't exist. You have foretold the future. Do not deny it."

"I have spoken the truth. I'm not hiding anything. There is no future, but—"

"But? But what?"

"There is no single future, but there are *futures*."

The king leaned toward the sightless man, sensing he was finally getting to the point. "Go on," he said.

Uzzi sighed. "Think of life as a vast web of roads, more intricate and complicated than any spider's silken snare. Every decision stands at a fork in the road. It may break three ways, or three thousand. The possibilities are often numerous, but never infinite. Of course there too many futures for any mere mortal to discern, but God sees them all, and he knows which one we will choose."

"So man is destined by fate."

"No! Are your eyes so clear that you have forgotten how to listen? Are there really so many bootlickers surrounding you that you have lost the ability to understand another person's thoughts?"

Joshabad stared menacingly at the blind man. "You forget your place, seer."

Uzzi breathed in slowly, then said, "There is no fate. The futures are certain, but the future is never decided."

"Stop beating around the bush! Tell me, how do you know what will be?"

"God knows every one of us intimately, from the heart, better than we know ourselves. He also knows that impossibly complicated web of possible futures. He sees every crossroad before us and knows where each road leads after that. When you accept these two facts, the rest is simple."

"Not so simple as you make it out to be, seer."

"Suppose you, the king, are awakened by the trumpets' alarm in the middle of the night. An enemy has surprised you and laid siege to the city. You must take decisive action. There are numerous possibilities, more than your small mind can possibly imagine..."

The king issued a warning by clearing his throat.

Uzzi ignored the threat. "In his divine omniscience, God knows which of the myriad futures you will choose. You see, *you* are predictable. The future, which doesn't exist, is not. That is why I say three know what will be. God, because he knows all futures and those who must choose from them; I, because He whispers in my ear; and the one to whom the future belongs, because he chooses it."

The king said nothing for a long time. Uzzi sat in the silence comfortably, accustomed to the dark. Finally, the king revealed why he had summoned his guest. "Uzzi, tell me. What will become of me?"

"If you truly believe I can tell you this, O king, then take my advice. Do not ask me to divine what lies ahead. At the moment there are many possibilities. Let that be enough."

"The priest was right—you are a troublemaker! It is not enough. I must know. I cannot focus, cannot sleep. Tell me, Uzzi. Tell me what will become of me, or else—I swear it—I will deliver you over to the torturers who will stripe your back. I will have you beaten until either you tell me, or you have no breath to do so!"

"You leave me no choice," said Uzzi. "I will tell you what you want to know. But just remember—I warned you not to coerce me to tell."

"Speak, seer. Tell what is to be."

"Your fears will soon be confirmed. You, O king, shall be a leper! Your skin shall fade white until it remains as pale as I'm sure you are now, and you shall cover your face and wander the earth in exile. You shall hang as a ghost betwixt life and death, until mercy releases your pitiful spirit, and you are finally gathered to your fathers."

"I knew it," said the king in a whisper. "Somehow I knew it." He rose from his throne and paced around the room in deep thought. "You said I choose my future, did you not?"

The blind man's shoulders slumped. "I did."

"So tell me this, seer, and I will let you go back to whatever miserable cave they dragged you out of. Is it too late? Have I already sealed my fate?"

"How is it that a man with the mind of an infant can rule a kingdom? Do you still not understand? Do my shriveled eyes see better than yours? You have no fate! You are shaping your own dreadful end. Even now, by asking this question, you are doing it. I speak not of fate, yet what I foretell is inevitable. For you will always be you, king, and there is nothing you can do to stop it."

"We'll see about that," said Joshabad.

The next day, the king set out for the high places in Bethel. When he arrived, the priest performed the ceremony for the cleansing of leprous disease. Dressed in white linen robes, he took a dove in his left hand, and held its head between the knuckles of his right hand and pulled off its head over a bowl of fresh water. He held the warm, twitching body over the bowl and squeezed the blood into it. He then added cedarwood, scarlet yarn, and hyssop. Then he took a second bird and dipped it into the bowl until it was wet with the water and the blood of its companion and released it. He lifted the hyssop out of the bowl and flicked it toward the king seven times, sprinkling him with the bloody water. After pronouncing him clean, the priest ordered that he be shaved from head to toe. After shaving, the king bathed and dressed himself in new clothes. Then he returned home, bald and clean. A week later he returned to Bethel with two male lambs and a ewe and fine flour mixed with oil to complete the offerings. When he returned to his throne to resume his duties, the king felt clean for the first time since he had returned from his journey.

The court physicians examined him and assured him of his good health, taking oaths upon their lives and the lives of their children that the king had not been afflicted by leprosy and that his skin was as clear as newly fallen snow. The queen scoffed at the words of Uzzi, remarking that his mind was as blind as his eyes. Other prophets gladly contradicted Uzzi's words, and soon the king began to doubt them himself, forgetting how piercing they were at the time and how reluctantly they were shared.

The day after his second trip from Bethel, before the hair had begun to grow back on his head, he called for Huri, the captain of his army. "I want you to return to the leper colony we found on the way home from Rabbah," he said, "kill every miserable wretch that lives there, and burn it to the ground until every last trace of it is gone. Then I want you to scour the kingdom. Find all the lepers living within the borders of Israel and put them to death—man, woman, or child, no matter how severe or how minor the disease."

Huri started with the leper colony they had encountered by the river when they wandered from the trade route. His men dragged every leper, wraithlike and moaning, into the middle of the camp and put them to death by the sword. They killed the children first in a gesture of mercy, so they would not have to watch the others die. As the cold executioners worked, the haunting sound of the lepers' moaning grew fainter and fainter, until there was only one old woman left. Then they cut her down, and it was quiet. They set the lepers' tents and the rest of their possessions on fire, and a black plume rose out of the valley like a demon hoard riding into the sky. They worked their way from there to the rest of the kingdom, killing every leper from Dan to Beersheba, those who bore the signs of the disease and even those who were merely rumored to have it. The land groaned under their swords, for the king's healing was severe, and widows and orphans filled the land.

Thirty days after he had stumbled upon the leper colony, the king felt better than ever. No signs of the disease could be found in his body. His skin was clear, his energy high. He was certain he had changed his fate, if Uzzi's words were even to be believed.

He had delayed celebrations upon his return because he had been too distracted to feast. But now he could focus on the future. The leper colony was a distant memory; it felt more like a dream to him than a reality.

A banquet had been prepared in his honor in the Great Hall of the palace. City leaders, priests, government officials, advisors, and soldiers engorged themselves on platters full of dates, pomegranates, grapes, figs, roasted lamb, and bread. The wine flowed freely, and many of the revelers were already drunk. Musicians, singers, and dancing girls entertained the guests. Joshabad sat at the head of the long table as his guests, one after another, showered him with praise.

"No king in Israel has ever governed with such equity and peace," one said.

"The kingdom has never known such lasting peace," said another.

"May your wife bear you ten princes!"

The king received every blessing heartily and without reservation. After all, the kingdom was in good shape. He deserved the accolades. It had been a difficult three months. Why shouldn't he receive his guests' praise and enjoy the fruits of his toil?

The king stood. The sound of the lyre and the singers stopped abruptly. The guests quieted their brash and tawdry communications. All eyes turned to the anointed leader at the head of the table.

"I would like to raise a toast," said the king, lifting his goblet high in the air. "First, to my priest and those who serve with him at the high places in Bethel, for your prayers on my behalf, without which I would not stand here in good health before these loyal subjects."

The priest, wet-lipped and rosy-cheeked, smiled and dipped his balding head in a practiced bow.

"Next, to the captain of my army, might right-hand man, Huri, for your constant dedication, and to the army he leads, the fiercest company of fighting men Israel has ever known!"

The room erupted in cheers, and the soldiers shouted and slapped one another on the back. Huri, for his part, maintained his usual expressionless stare. If he was enjoying himself, it did not show in his countenance.

"Finally, to my wife, the queen. There is no match for your beauty and your grace. May we rule Israel together, and may our children become—"

A sudden crash interrupted the king's toast, and he felt something cold splash against his lower legs and feet. A hush fell over the guests, and Joshabad felt their eyes on him, staring not at his face, which continued grinning absently as he tried to discern the source of the noise that had interrupted his speech, but at the arm he had extended to hold the goblet as he made his toast. Slowly, the king traced their stares to his hand, which was still cupped and held aloft, only it was empty. He had dropped the goblet and had not even felt it slip from his grasp.

All eyes watched the king as he withdrew his hand, taking it in the other, which he used to massage the muscles in his palm and stretch the fingers. There was no feeling in it. The goblet had not merely slipped out of his hand. He dropped it because the hand he had used to hold it aloft was weak and no longer had sensitivity.

An invisible dagger plunged through him as he recalled the words of the blind prophet—*You shall be a leper!* He did his best to recover his former demeanor. "Musicians, play us a song!" he said, forgetting his toast. The lyrist obediently began to strum, and the singers sang, but the eyes did not break their stare. "Excuse me while I confer briefly with my captain," he said, looking over at Huri. "Please continue. There is plenty of wine." He forced a smile, then turned and exited the banquet hall with the stolid army captain hot on his heels.

When they were out of earshot from the party, the king hissed at his captain: "You told me you had purged leprosy from the land!"

"I d-did, my king! I saw to it that every last one of those miserable wretches were put to the sword!" Huri, who was usually imperturbable, stammered as he tried to defend himself.

"How, then, do you explain this?" Joshabad held the numb hand before Huri's face. He had not noticed it before, but now he could see that it was blanched, and the nails had begun to yellow and separate from his fingers.

"I-I can't, my lord. I eliminated every one of them, just as you said."

Joshabad's eye caught a glimpse of something on the captain's forearm, something red like slaughtered lamb. He had noticed earlier that Huri had been standing in the corner with that arm tucked out of sight. Quickly, the king snatched the arm up so that he could examine it in the torchlight flickering in the palace halls.

White scales, dry like the skin of a fish dried by the sun, covered the greater portion of his forearm.

"So it's you."

Huri fell on his face before the king, the two of them bound by a slow, pale death. "I swear it!" he cried. "I didn't know until yesterday morning!"

"Say no more, captain. I brought this about. If anyone is to blame, it is your king. The prophet was right. I chose this path. We returned from Rabbah clean. The only leprosy we brought home was smuggled in my imagination. That is, until I sent you back. You picked up the foul plague on your return, when you slaughtered those poor beggars by the river.

From that day forward, the king lived in quarantine by the river at the place where he encountered the lepers on his journey back from Rabbah. He had a modest dwelling built there upon the ashes of the former colony he had ordered his armies to incinerate, and in doing so, brought about the very outcome he had so desperately wished to avoid.

The king had plenty of time to reflect on his life while he was there. There was little more to do than think as he waited on death to take him one piece at a time. He thought about the blind prophet and how foolish he had been to ignore him. He also thought about how most of his life he had blamed fate for all the disappointments and the trials and how he had taken credit for the triumphs and the plunder. But all that time he had been responsible for all of it, while the Lord watched from his celestial throne, knowing what he would do before he did it. All his life he blamed others for his misfortunes, or he blamed God, but now he realized that he had been climbing a spiral staircase of his own making, one that rose high and then stopped midair, ending nowhere.

Finally, more from a desire for breathable air than curiosity about what lay inside the wall, the foot obeyed its master's command and stepped into the breach.

The Breach

Mind your words, tread carefully, little one. See the stars? What are they? Do you know? Lights in the sky? Holes awled into God's shroud, letting his glory poke through? Nay, my child, I will tell you. They are angels! Their light reaches all the way from heaven to our humble earth, observing all our ways. They burn brighter at night as a reminder that not even darkness hides our creaturely deeds. Always mind your ways. The Watchers see, and their liminal voices have the ear of God.

1

Eli was starving. It had been twenty-four days since he and the others fled the city through the breach in the wall. They found shelter in a rocky outcropping eight or nine miles from the city and had been surviving on whatever food they were able to scavenge—hares, lizards, small birds, and a donkey someone had sacrificed for the group—unclean, yes, but how can a man follow the law when he is dead?

Eli didn't know how many had tried to follow him out of the city. Swords and spears cut their ranks in half, at least, on their way through the wall, and now there were maybe a hundred survivors left, all of them looking to him for guidance.

The hunger gnawing at his belly was bad enough, but the guilt he felt over abandoning the city was seven times worse. At night, sounds of the enemy's celebrations echoed throughout the camp. He could hear them looting homes, and sometimes he heard the awful screams of women whose sons and husbands had been killed in the invasion. He thought about the startled gasps of the man who had been running beside him when a soldier's spear impaled him, and he winced. Even this far out, the air was thick with smoke from the buildings they had set on fire. Sleep evaded him most nights, and then when he managed to drift off, nightmares plagued his head with visions of unspeakable atrocities committed against the men, women, and children he had left behind. Why are we capable of tormenting ourselves with our worst fears, even in our sleep?

As a young man, Eli thought the world was something a man could control. His parents made sure he received the finest education possible. He had been married and dreamed of a house full of children. The king himself more than once called for his administrative talents. But somewhere along the way, everything fell apart. Unlike other men who gradually came to realize their own futility through daily frustrations, Eli's sense of competence crumbled all at once when his wife fell ill with the sickness that would eventually take her life. He had been angry with God for taking her, but now he was beginning to think her untimely death had been an act of mercy.

He had to stop second-guessing himself. They had been right to run away. By the second new moon of the siege, Eli knew they had lost the city and it was only a matter of time before the enemy breached the wall. He wished more had followed his lead. Better to escape than to sit around waiting for execution. Even if the wall had not been breached, they would have died from starvation within days. He had not realized how quickly the enemy's swords could sweep so many of them away during their escape, but still about a hundred of them were left, a hundred who may not have survived another night in the captured city.

The way he saw it, they had only two options. They could not stay where they were. There was too little water and no food. They were too exposed. It would not be long before marauding nomads descended upon them like vultures on a cadaverous feast. No, they couldn't stay put. The only two choices were, one, head north for Gibeah in hopes of finding asylum, unless the enemy had already destroyed them too, or, two, risk reentering the city on the off chance the enemy had finished its murdering and looting and abandoned it for their next conquest. There was no way of knowing which choice, if either, ended in safety. But they couldn't stay where they were.

A woman's voice startled him from his reverie. "Eli, my little boy is starving. He hasn't eaten in three days." It was Maacah, whose husband had been among the fallen during their escape.

"I know," said Eli sympathetically, "everyone is starving, Maacah. What do you want me to do about it?"

"Someone has to do something. We can't just die out here."

"There are worse places to die. Do you want to go back to the city? Did you hear the screams? Do you know what soldiers do to young women like you? If worse comes to worse, and you die from starvation or heat exhaustion, you should thank me for it."

Maacah looked down at the ground, searching for her words.

Eli watched the top of her head for a moment, then spoke: "I have a plan. It has been very quiet out there for the last several days. Have you noticed?"

"Yes, much quieter than at first."

"Well, I've been thinking. This wasn't a takeover so much as it was a show of power. They don't want to live in Jerusalem. They just want to show us who's boss. You know, break some things, tear a hole in the wall, loot the temple, and kill a few hundred people so that we'll keep paying tribute. Right?"

"I suppose," said Maacah. She didn't seem too sure.

"What would it hurt if we got a closer look, just to see if they went back home? I could leave in the morning before sunrise and be back before noon. If the hostiles are still there, we run to Gibeah, but if they're gone, maybe we can return home and rebuild our lives."

Maacah hung her head.

"Look," said Eli, putting his hand on her shoulder, "I know you lost someone. He was a good man. I know how you feel. It will never be the same, but think about your son."

She nodded.

"Get some rest. Tomorrow I'll put eyeballs on the city, and after I'm able to find out what's going on over there, we'll break camp and go in one direction or the other."

On the outside, Eli may have looked confident, in control, but inside his guts were twisting like a nest full of snakes. Most of the men thought he'd lost his mind when he told them his plan. He tended to agree with them, but the way he saw it, they were half dead from starvation anyway. If they got killed trying to reenter the city, they were merely sparing themselves from withering away in the wilderness.

That night, Eli lay on his back and watched the stars. An eccentric uncle of his, his mother's brother, used to tell stories about the heavens. He liked to say the stars were angels watching the earth from their celestial vantage point. He told Eli they shined more brightly at night because that's when people think no one's looking. Any fool who thinks he can hide in the darkness will change his mind if he looks up at the night sky and realizes the stars are God's angels, he said. Even as a child, Eli doubted his uncle's astronomical speculations, but now he was especially skeptical. It was hard not to believe that he and the others had been forgotten in the wilderness. He had never felt so alone. How had he become the head of a band of skeletal refugees in this parched wilderness?

Fire flew across the sky above him, illuminating the sleeping faces of those who were lying around him. A shooting star. It covered his entire line of sight, from horizon to horizon. *How many times a night does a star blaze across the night sky unnoticed,* he wondered as he looked at the sleeping bodies around him, oblivious to the heavenly machinations above them. They slept during the day too, a different kind of sleep, exhausting, not restorative, a kind of oblivion the mind uses to shield itself from the horrors of reality. Most people know only a sliver of what happens around them, yet God expects them to use wisdom and decide the best course for themselves and their families. No wonder life so often ends in tragedy. We grope blindly in darkness.

And the stars? he heard his uncle interject.

Yes, the stars, thought Eli. *Such cold light for a sign*.

2

The next morning, Eli rose early and headed toward the city, following the smoke rising from the structures the invading army had torched. Getting eyes on the walls without being detected would be tricky. He had to be careful. If there were hostiles on the wall, he would be able to see them in time to beat a hasty retreat without being spotted. But if the wall was clear, he would have to approach the city for a closer look. The motions of his plan were simple, but Eli struggled to compose himself against the abject terror he felt with every step he took in the direction of the wall. With tremendous effort, he willed himself forward, trying not to think about what would happen if he got caught.

He followed the black pillar of smoke, its pungent smell filling his head. Although it danced before him in the wind like a solitary tower, he knew it grew from dozens of homes, shops, and government buildings on fire, maybe more. And somewhere in that dark flume the temple's remains escaped into the atmosphere, as if God were calling it home.

After three hours, he came within sight of the wall. All was quiet as far as he could see. Nothing moved. The city sat on a high hill, and the wind howled in the higher elevation. Tumbleweeds rolled across the plain between him and the wall. He saw the breach that had opened their city, a gate of destruction belching smoke like the furnaces of hell. It was in the shape of a wedge, wider at the top and narrow toward the bottom. The opening was smaller than Eli remembered, and he marveled that he and the other survivors in his party had been able to escape. Bodies littered the ground around the opening where the hostiles had struck them down. They had been lying there for three weeks, exposed to the elements and wild animals. Eli cursed the hostiles for their cruelty. Could they not have at least tossed the bodies into a mass grave?

Maacah's husband was there, and many others who had tried to follow Eli out of the city.

Eli made a square of vision by overlapping his hands and peered through it, trying to see farther. Nothing but silent walls, the bodies of the dead, and billowing smoke. Maybe the hostiles had returned home, leading away the survivors as captives. He scratched his disheveled beard and swallowed hard. He couldn't be sure from this far away. There was no way around it. He would have to enter the breach to get a closer look.

The breach's mouth gaped open, either mocking or beckoning him, Eli wasn't sure. He would have to cover two hundred yards of open ground before he reached it. If the hostiles were still in there, they'd dispatch him with an arrow before he got very far, but what else could he do? Everyone back at the camp looked to him for guidance. He had to find out who, if anyone, was behind that wall.

Eli picked out some scrub fifty yards ahead and ran for it, staying low. He dove for cover when he reached it, scraping his knees on the loose chert of the desert floor. His heart was pounding out of his chest. He peered over the leaves of the brush he was hiding behind. No shouts or arrows flying through the air. Eli was beginning to accept that the city might really be abandoned.

While he stooped in his hiding place, catching his breath, he surveyed his surroundings, and his eye fell upon the decomposing body of one of his fallen comrades. It lay supine, staring at the sky from black, empty sockets. Eli remembered how he contemplated the sky the night before and wondered if the man had died thinking about the silent angels.

Another hundred yards or so, and he would be standing in the breach. He took a deep breath, trying to slow his pounding heart, and focused on the smoking hole in the wall. Then, having cleared his mind of every thought except for reaching the wall, he darted out from his scrub cover and sprinted toward the breach.

He came to a full stop at the wall. Standing in front of the breach, he could see nothing but black smoke. It stung his eyes and filled his lungs, and he doubled over, coughing uncontrollably. The only way to discover what or who lay within those walls was by running blindly through the breach's black curtain. The wall was approximately nine feet wide here. He could span it in four or five steps.

Eli commanded his right foot to take the first step, but it refused, frozen by fear. Finally, more from a desire for breathable air than curiosity about what lay inside the wall, the foot obeyed its master's command and stepped into the breach.

One step, four more.

The second step landed on something soft, a body probably. Eli felt sick, and he could barely breathe because of the breach's acrid atmosphere. He fought the urge to turn back and took another step.

The air suddenly sweetened and a fierce gust nearly blew him off his feet. Debris circulated in the air above him. Dust bit his eyes, and he had to lean forward to stay on his feet. Why did the wind pick up? Did the breach somehow funnel the air currents through the wall?

No turning back now. Two more steps—

The next step seemed to take him into a whole new place, as if the breach had compressed layers of experience into the small space it inhabited. The wind stopped as quickly as it began. Eli heard voices and other sounds he couldn't place, like trumpets on feast days and low growls or stones rolling. A celebration? The noise of the city's survivors, rejoicing over the enemy's departure? Eli had carefully contained his hope since the siege began, but now he cautiously allowed it to poke its head out from the fragile veil of his heart and look around. He listened intently while rubbing his eyes and blinking, trying to see through the black smoke. Bracing himself for whatever came next, he took one final step out from the smoking plume to get his first look at the city since the invasion.

The smoke cleared immediately. No, cleared wasn't the word for it. Rather, it *vanished* completely as if it had never existed. The morning light shined brightly in his eyes, and Eli's senses suddenly became overwhelmed with new sights and sounds. Something sped toward him on his left, and he stumbled wildly backward, just in time to avoid being struck by it. He coughed in the noxious fumes it left in its wake and watched it roll down the street and disappear around the corner—a bright blue horseless chariot! He rolled over onto all fours to stand, expecting to see the breach he had just emerged from, but instead of the breach's smoking mouth, he saw a row of glass doors. He gaped at his own shocked image in the door directly in front of him. Above it a sign dangled bearing two red roses and letters woven with thorn-laden stems that read FLOWERS.

Where did the wall go? And the breach—

"Get out of the sidewalk, dopehead!" A voice growled maliciously above him. Eli realized he had fallen backward into a paved walkway, upsetting the flow of pedestrians, many of whom had to walk around or step over him as they passed. He rose to his feet, dusting himself off, his heart pounding from his near miss with the chariot, and reeling with confusion over the absence of the breach and the strange world he had stepped into. The crowd shoving their way around him could not have been Israelites or hostiles. They were dressed unlike any people he had ever seen before. A few of the women wore tunics and robes, but the rest covered their legs with sleeves, like the arms of a tunic, only tighter. Some of the women walked alone through the streets with their long, brown legs completely exposed. All of them painted their faces, and some had dyed their fingernails and toenails. Eli diverted his eyes. These women could make the harlots blush back home. Strange, heathen tattoos decorated arms, legs, and necks.

How could this be Jerusalem? Where was he? Was he dreaming? He must have been dreaming!

Everything was all wrong. He entered the door of the flower shop where the breach had been, praying that it opened to the familiar surroundings of the land outside the wall of his home in Jerusalem. A bell rang behind him as he stepped into a bright, flower-spangled room. White light buzzed from long cylinders lining the ceiling, and flowers decorated the tables and shelves all over the room. Wreaths hung on the walls. He saw only one person in the crowded space, a young, attractive woman shifting uncomfortably on a stool behind a counter.

3

Eli approached the counter of the flower shop unsure how to begin. He wanted to talk to the woman, but he got the impression she didn't want to be bothered. Her face looked even more harried than his.

"Excuse me," he tried in Hebrew.

The woman behind the counter seemed lost in a daydream. She stared at something over Eli's shoulder. He couldn't tell what.

"Excuse me?" he said more loudly this time.

She inhaled suddenly through her nose as if she had just been awakened from a deep sleep and turned, noticing him for the first time. "Oh—I'm sorry," she said as she nervously smoothed her hair and shifted on her stool behind the counter.

Relieved that she seemed to understand him, he said, "Yes, I—So, let's see—I'm not really sure where to start."

What if she were one of them? Maybe he passed out while crossing the breach and had been asleep for a long time, long enough for them to have replaced his people with hers, so they could occupy the city with their shameful clothes and smoking horseless chariots. He had to be careful, find out what had happened without revealing too much.

"Are you looking for bouquets?" she said, suddenly filled with new energy. "Maybe something for your director and the producers?" She sprang out of her seat and floated over to a display rack filled with spring bouquets in buckets of water. She selected a couple of arrangements to show Eli, who stared at her slackjawed while she kept speaking. "Oh, but you must not forget the poor stage manager and the costume designer. Nobody ever remembers them! Although—" She spun around and studied his tunic while stroking her chin. "I'm not too sure she deserves much recognition for *that*."

"Producers?"

"Yes—you're an actor, no? In a play?"

Eli squinted and shook his head. What was this woman going on about? He had to learn what had happened. "What has happened to the city?" he said.

His tone startled her. Her eyes grew large, and her face remembered its troubled expression. She returned the bouquets to their places on the rack and reclaimed her stool, putting the counter between herself and the strange man standing in her shop wearing a tattered tunic.

"Where did the northern hoard go?" he said.

The woman wrinkled her brow and looked up at him with a frown. "What'd you say?"

"The invaders, the siege—they breached the wall. Where did they all go?"

The woman pushed away from her counter as far as her stool would allow. Eli could tell he had startled her. For the last several months he had felt like prey, but now he felt like a deadly hunter, seeing her shrink away from him like that. He caught a glimpse of himself, filthy and disheveled, in a mirror on the wall and realized how imposing and strange he must have seemed to her. "Please, I mean no harm. I don't know what has happened." His voice trailed in a quaver.

She softened a little. Her eyes turned soft and brown. They conjured up an image in Eli's mind of Aila in happier days, running in a golden field, grain waist-high, wide as the world. She laughed as she ran to him. He opened his arms to hold her small frame. The heads of grain drifted in the wind and became her eyes, her dark brown eyes.

Eli willed himself out of his daydream and looked at the living woman before him. Her eyes were scared, perplexed. They pointed toward his but fixed on something beyond him, on a place he could not see. Her thoughts seemed to be racing faster than his.

"Let's start over," she said and tried to smile. "My name's Beth. What's yours?"

"Eli."

"Eli." There was something comforting about hearing her say his name. "Now, why don't you start by telling me about yourself, like where you're from and why you're here. Are you not an actor or something?" She examined his long, unkept beard and tattered tunic.

"I've come from the wilderness. I don't know—I'm lost."

"Yes," she said. Her head turned toward the center of the shop. "I've been feeling a little lost myself today."

"No, I mean I really don't know where I am."

Beth furrowed her brow and studied the man in her shop for a moment. "Here," she said as she pulled a folded document from a stack that lay on the counter and spread it out so Eli could read it. It was a map, the detail and coloring more brilliant than any writing he had ever seen. When he leaned over to look at it more closely, he noticed that her hair smelled like almond blossoms.

"This is a map of the old city of Jerusalem. We're here, in the Jewish quarter."

"Jewish?"

"Yes, silly, Jewish, you know, like Abraham, Moses, and the Israelites. King David, Anne Frank, Woody Allen. *Jews*, you know."

Eli stared at the map in stunned silence. "I have never heard my people called by that name before."

Beth's face contracted again. She paused as if she were having second thoughts about having this conversation, then returned her attention to the map. "Over here's the Muslim quarter, here's the Christian quarter, and here's the Armenian quarter. And here's the Temple Mount."

"The temple?" Eli said hopefully. "Can you take me there? To the temple?"

Beth laughed. "Well, it's not like I can take you to the *temple.* I can take you to where it *was.*" Eli's heart sank. Of course! The hostiles must have razed the temple during the siege.

The bell at the door announced the entrance of a well-dressed, young couple. Beth smiled toward them as they entered. They smiled back, then they looked at Eli, who was speaking to Beth, oblivious that someone else had entered the room. Their smiles dropped when they saw him, and they diverted their attention to the rack of bouquets.

Eli focused his attention upon Beth. Her shoulder-length, black hair was held back by an amber-colored plait, and she wore a simple, white button-down blouse and sleeve coverings on her legs. Her lips were full and red. A thin, silver chain hung around her slender neck holding a pendant in the shape of a cross. He had never seen jewelry like that before. Did it signify something special in this place? He stared at it for a second but quickly shifted his gaze, blushing because it rested against her skin. Talking to an unfamiliar woman in public made him uncomfortable. His instincts told him to run, but he fought the urge to retreat and tried to concentrate.

After an uncomfortably long silence, she said, "Why are you dressed like that? It looks like you've come from play practice."

Eli looked down at his soiled, tattered tunic and rubbed it self-consciously, then looked back up at her, confused. "They're a little dirty. I have been living in the wilderness with the others for the last twenty-five days."

"The others? What others? Where are they now?"

"In the wilderness." He pointed at the place where the smoking breach had been, which was now a plaster wall displaying wreaths of flowers. "We fled the city during the siege, and we have been surviving in the wilderness for twenty-five days. I came to see if the hostiles had cleared out, hoping we might be able to return."

The couple, who couldn't help overhearing their conversation, shot an alarmed look in their direction. The young man seized his companion by the arm and led her out the door.

Beth gave Eli an annoyed look. "What siege? And where's this wilderness you're talking about? Who are you, Rip Van Winkle? You act like you've been sleeping for a thousand years."

"So is that it? Are you working with them? Did they put me to sleep like this Torn Winkle fellow and replace my people with harlots and horseless chariots?" Eli's emotions were rising, and he leaned over the counter, shouting these conspiracies at Beth, who almost fell off her stool trying to create space between herself and this madman who had burst through her door a few moments earlier.

"You need help!" she yelled.

"That's what I've been trying to tell you!"

"Why don't you find the rest of your David and Goliath friends, go back to play practice, and leave me alone? I've got enough to worry about without you running off my customers, standing here in your stinky shepherd outfit, and wasting my time!"

"You don't understand! I—"

"I think you should go."

Eli bitterly snatched up the map from the counter and stormed out, nearly breaking his arm trying to push the door open.

"Pull," barked Beth.

Eli yanked the door open and went outside.

4

Eli stood on the sidewalk outside the flower shop examining his map. Beth had pointed out where they were—the Jewish quarter. According to the map, the wall wasn't where he had come out of the flower shop, but several hundred feet away. Eli made his way over to it, the map guiding him, and tried not to get distracted by the unusual sights and sounds surrounding him. He learned quickly to respect the horseless chariots. They did not stop for pedestrians. Also, he had to do something about his clothes. His appearance drew a lot of unwanted attention. He studied the people milling along the street, not relishing the idea of dressing to match their styles. The clothes they wore looked tight, and the thought of wearing them made him feel embarrassed. But he didn't know how long he would be here, or if he would ever escape, so he would have to do his best to fit in, which meant finding some new clothes as soon as possible.

The wall was not at all what he expected. Not only was it in the wrong place, it was narrower and twice as tall. The stones comprising it were smaller than he remembered, and the top was lined with battlements. He also spied several watchtowers he could not recognize.

An overweight man with a red goatee wearing a brown wide-brimmed hat led a group of elderly people along the wall. He had a pack strapped to his back, and he was talking incessantly, gesturing toward the wall as he did so. At intervals, the crowd looked at one another and smiled and nodded, pleased with what he was saying.

"Suleiman ordered that the walls should have thirty-four watchtowers and seven gates. Construction lasted approximately four years and concluded in 1541. They are almost two and a half miles long and encompass a third of a square mile."

Eli eavesdropped on the man's presentation. He was too far away to hear every word, but he learned enough to complicate the mysterious riddle he'd fallen into. What did the heavyset man mean by 1541? Was that a date? When was that? Eli waited until the man finished answering questions and the crowd dissipated, then he approached him warily. He knew his appearance would raise questions, but he had to take the chance.

"I'm sorry, I don't have any cash on me," the man said, dismissing Eli with a wave.

"I don't want your silver. Can I ask you about the wall?"

The man cast a doubtful glance in Eli's direction. "Well, the tour is over, and I was about to get some lunch. I can give you five minutes. What do you want to know?"

"Who fixed the wall?"

"Who fixed the wall when?"

"The wall was breached, it's different now, who fixed the wall?"

"Look, sir, if you want me to answer your question, you have to be more specific. Slow down and tell me who exactly do you mean breached the wall."

"The northern hoard."

"Ah. You must mean the Neo-Babylonian Empire. Yes, that breach was not repaired for 150 years until Nehemiah in 444 B.C.E."

"So this man, Nehemiah, he built all this?"

"No—" The man frowned. "Three hundred years after Nehemiah, the Hasmoneans expanded the walls, which Herod the Great elaborated upon 100 years later. Then the Romans destroyed those walls and rebuilt them in the third and fourth centuries C.E. These were destroyed by earthquakes. Saladin reinforced them around 1,200 C.E., and finally the Ottomans built these walls in the sixteenth century C.E. Does that answer your question?"

Eli stared numbly at the tour guide. This man threw out centuries of time as if he were eternity itself. "So how many years from the Babylonians were these walls?"

The man wore a satisfied smile on his pudgy face. "Oh, about 1,900 years, give or take."

The ground beneath Eli's feet buckled and swayed, and the horizon shifted forty-five degrees. He broke out in a cold sweat and moaned involuntarily.

"Say, buddy, are you alright?"

A dark hood slowly fell over Eli's vision, and he passed out cold and fell onto the pavement.

Eli woke up in a dimly lit room, lying on cool, white sheets under a soft blanket. The last thing he remembered was talking to the heavyset man on the sidewalk near the wall, then everything went dark. The man told him something—he couldn't remember what. His head was pounding too hard for him to think. Where was he now? He could tell he was in a room in a large building. He heard voices, some urgent, some casual, and unworldly high-pitched tones. Other sounds—heavy rolling objects, the forceful venting of air, a man crying for help, the revolting suctioning of viscous fluids—resonated throughout this place. He craned his neck around the railing of the bed where he lay and saw a window through which he spotted the tops of trees, houses, and tall buildings. The room he was in must have been several stories above ground. He rotated his head around and saw a box looming over him, beside his head on the left side of the bed. The box was covered with lights and strange characters, and it whirled and beeped in his ear, as if it were some strange idol trying to communicate heresies. A transparent cord trailed away from it. His eyes followed it until it ended—in his hand! Eli's breathing quickened. He panicked and pushed himself up in the bed, kicking the bedding and whimpering pitifully through his nose which made him aware of more cording wrapped around his face and going into his nostrils. He grasped the cord connected to his hand tightly and was about to yank it out of his body to keep whatever it was from entering him when a soft hand fell upon his arm.

A woman's voice— "Shh. You're okay."

Eli turned his head to the other side of the bed to see who it was and found himself looking into the brown eyes of the woman from the flower shop.

"You—what are you doing here? Where am I?"

She removed her hand from his arm and eased back into the chair beside the bed. She spoke in a soothing tone. "It's going to be okay. You passed out in the street, and they've taken you to a hospital. You've been asleep for almost twenty-four hours."

Eli's eyes slowly left hers and surveyed the room as he tried to process what she had told him. Then he remembered the cord stuck in his hand. He looked at it, his face twisting in panic.

"Leave it alone. They're giving you fluids by IV. You were severely malnourished."

Eli laid back and tried to believe her, unable to take his mind off the fluid dripping from the box into his veins. "Why are you here? I mean, how did you find me?"

"Zozo."

"Zozo?"

"Well, after I closed the shop, I saw Zozo sitting cross-legged on the ground, cradling someone in his lap and fanning him with his hat. That someone turned out to be you. I went over to see what was going on, called an ambulance, and here you are."

"Who's Zozo?"

"The tour guide," she said. "He said you were asking all these questions about the wall, how old it was and who built it, and then all of the sudden you collapsed onto the sidewalk."

Eli now remembered what the tour guide had said. *About 1,900 years, give or take.* The words set off alarms in his nervous system, and he began to shiver, more from panic than cold. "H—Have you been here the whole time?"

"I must have stumbled on you two right after you fainted." She stifled a snicker by making a loose fist under her nose. "I think he thought you had died! His face was bright red, and he kept praying, 'Lord, don't take him! Please, Lord, don't take him!'" Her words broke into laughter. Then she noticed Eli shivering and gasped. "You poor thing! Are you cold? I'm so sorry! I'm laughing while you're freezing to death in that thin hospital gown."

Eli glanced under the blanket and noticed he was nearly naked, which didn't help his nerves.

"I think there's another blanket." Beth jumped up from her chair and rummaged through a wooden cabinet on the wall. That was when Eli noticed an olive-skinned boy, about nine, who had been sitting behind Beth on an easy chair in the corner of the room, bent over and working furiously on something in his lap with a pencil.

Beth returned with the blanket and spread it over Eli's gaunt frame.

"Who's that?" Eli gestured toward the boy in the corner.

"That's my son, Joshua."

Eli watched her and waited for her to elaborate.

"Just the two of us." She said this while fussing with the blanket in a manner that suggested to Eli that he should stop prying and change the subject.

The blanket helped, but he was still shivering. He stared at the wall in front of him. A white board covered with colorful markings was mounted next to a flat rectangular black glass. Cords trailed from the glass into the wall. Cords everywhere, coming out of boxes, running into walls, into him.

Beth hooked a bag around her shoulder and remained standing. "Listen, I've got to go. Is there anyone I can call for you?

Family, friends, someone who can look after you until you get back on your feet?"

"I'm all by myself," he said sullenly, "like I told you before."

Beth shifted her gaze to the floor for an instant, then said, "Well then. Zozo said he'll be by later with some fresh clothes—they threw that old costume away. He'll help you get checked out, find someplace for you to stay till you get sorted out."

Eli looked up and managed a smile. "Thanks for staying with me."

"I'm glad you woke up."

"Me too, I think."

She turned toward the door, extending her hand for the boy to take it, but instead of running to his mother, he hopped up from the chair and scuttled over to Eli's bed with the sketch he had been feverishly drawing and handed it wordlessly to Eli, who accepted it as if it held the answers to the riddle that had been his life for the last day and a half, which, for all he knew, maybe it did. Eli examined the paper in his hand. It was see-through, like onion skin. On it was a connect-the-dot sketch of two crude dippers, a larger one at the bottom and a smaller upside-down one at the top. He recognized it as a drawing of the constellations Ursa Major and Ursa Minor, with Polaris at the tip of the handle.

Joshua ran to his mother, who smiled and tousled his hair. "He's obsessed with stars. He traces them out of his book."

"Thank you, Joshua. I will treasure it always."

The boy responded by giving Eli a shy grin and then followed his mother out of the room.

5

Zozo came, just as Beth had promised, sweeping into the room with a formal introduction, as if Eli were a foreign dignitary and he was on a diplomatic tour of his country. "Zozo Jubran, at your service." He brought Eli a pair of baggy cargo shorts and a colorful short-sleeved shirt decorated with palm leaves and large, white blossoms. Eli thought his new clothes looked ridiculous, but he noticed they matched Zozo's, so he withheld his protests and put them on. Zozo took him to a restaurant and fed him beef and lamb shawarma with couscous and pita, and Eli consumed it as if he were on the verge of starvation while Zozo watched with bemusement.

The kindly tour guide put Eli in a hostel in old Jerusalem where he could stay until he figured things out and bought him a few more flower print shirts and cargo shorts. Eli enjoyed strolling through the city with Zozo as his guide in the evenings. They walked through the plazas and alleyways, admiring the old structures lining the city's hills. Archways hung overhead, and ancient stones slept beneath his feet. Markets filled with bread, produce, lamb and beef kabobs, colorful bags for women, bright colorful clothing, ornate rugs, jewelry, and children's toys hummed with trade. Caper shrubs burrowed their roots into every crack they could find in rock retaining walls. As old as these structures were, none was standing in Eli's time. Compared to Eli, only the rocks were older, unless you counted the city itself.

Zozo also took Eli to the Western Wall, so he could see the remains of the temple. As the two men approached the Mughrabi Gate, Eli glimpsed an enormous golden dome rising from the highest point of the temple mount. Of all the changes he had witnessed since this bizarre ordeal began, this was by far the most shocking.

"Where is the temple? And what is that?"

"The temple's gone. That," Zozo said, pointing at the gold dome, "is the Dome of the Rock, the third holiest site in the world, according to the Muslims."

"Muslims? Who are the Muslims?"

"Boy, you really are out of touch," Zozo said, tugging on Eli's arm, "It's as if you've traveled in a time machine from the ancient past."

"Where are we going? I thought we were going to visit the temple mount."

"It's after 2:30. Jews are not allowed up there at this time of the day."

Eli jerked his face toward Zozo's. "No Jews on the temple mount?"

"Settle down. You're drawing attention to yourself."

"Why are you always so sheeplike? Nothing seems to rattle you. Where's your spine, huh? It's no wonder our people can no longer walk the streets of Jerusalem freely. We've laid down and allowed the enemies to take over."

For a moment, Eli thought maybe he had struck a nerve. Zozo gave him a troubled look, as if he were about to say something, but then the affable, rosy face returned, and he said, "Come on, there's something I want you to see."

Zozo dragged Eli past the Mughrabi Gate into a wide plaza filled with people. Eli immediately noticed a change in the attire. The clothing was looser and covered most of the skin, and most of the women wore head scarves. Some of the men wore black suits with round brimmed hats. Before them stretched a high wall of more familiar construction bordering the temple mount. It was ancient. Small, green caper shrubs grew out of cracks in the mortar. Near the wall, a barrier separated the men from the women. The people seemed to be praying before the wall. Some were weeping, some rocked back and forth, and others stuffed bits of paper into cracks in the wall. Eli surmised this was a holy place.

"The Western Wall, all that's left of the second temple. The people come here to pray for divine mercy and reflect upon God's blessings." Zozo had probably visited the wall hundreds of times, but he still spoke in soft, reverent tones.

Eli studied the ancient stones. All that was left of the holy dwelling place of God stood before him. "May I?" Eli asked.

Zozo responded by gesturing toward the wall.

Eli slipped off his sandals and approached the ancient structure. The crowd pressed him, and he could hear the supplicants murmuring their prayers around him. He reached out and lay his palm flat against the surface and felt its cool stones against his skin. He knew this wasn't the wall from his time, but at least it was old, and it was in the right place. He stood there with his hand pressed against it, eyes closed, for a long time. He felt connected, as if this wall somehow joined his past to the future. He remembered the suffering of his people and wondered how much more they had been through. He thought of the mosque upon the mount that had displaced the temple and the roaring engines of the horseless chariots that had replaced the lowing and bawling of sacrificial animals. He opened his eyes and saw the men on his right and left, praying their fervent prayers to God. *All this time, so much suffering, and yet we survived.* He had not prayed since he and the others escaped. Eli, like most people, neglected prayer when he needed it most. Maybe he had been too dehydrated before to cry, but now tears ran down his cheeks, and he thanked God for preserving his people through war, pestilence, and persecution. He also made a request: *Lord, I don't know how you can do it, but deliver me home. Send me back to my people in the wilderness. They're lost without me.*

He realized that he'd been thinking of those who survived the siege as if they shared his time and were just in a different space. In reality, they had died centuries ago. They shared approximately the same space, but not the same time. He was a lone survivor. To what end? Why had God brought him so far away from home?

Unlike Beth, Zozo seemed to be at ease with his awkwardness, but Eli soon grew tired of his curious nature. He asked too many questions. Not the questions he should have been asking, like, "Where did you come from?" or "Why are you dressed like a hermit?" or "How come you've never had falafel?" His questions pried into Eli's head. It was hard enough for one person to live in there, let alone two.

While strolling through the Christian district on one occasion, Zozo asked, "What is your favorite part of old Jerusalem?"

"The dogs. They're not like the ones back home that chew your leg off while you're sleeping."

Zozo chuckled. "Tell me, Eli, what do you want most out of life? Family? Friends? Power? Wealth? Mercy?"

"Say, why do you ask so many questions? You're always wanting to know if I like the food or what I think about some piece of music floating out of some random doorway. Why don't you mind your own business? I feel like I'm always taking a test."

"I'm just interested," Zozo said defensively.

"Look, I appreciate what you've done for me and all. Just stay out of my head, okay?"

"Whatever you say," Zozo said. He smirked as if he had no intention whatsoever of staying out of Eli's head.

"I want to ask you a question."

"Anything."

"What can you tell me about Beth?"

"Not much. I met her the same day I met you."

"You mean the two of you work on the same block and you never met until I passed out on the sidewalk?"

Zozo shrugged.

"And people wonder where I've been."

Eli lived in the hostel for nearly two weeks. He was far more comfortable there than he had been in the wilderness with the others, but thoughts of home did not fade from his mind. He could never fit in there. Even if he learned to follow the manners and customs of this new world, he'd merely be mimicking behavior, playing a part, unable to be himself. The longer he lingered as a foreigner in his own home, so far away, not in space, but in time, the more determined he was to return. If he only knew how.

6

Zozo and Eli often invited Beth to join them for dinner in the evenings, and having no one to leave him with, she always brought Joshua along. Zozo was very fond of the boy and called him the "ravager of walls." Eli caught the reference. The four of them could not have been more different, but somehow they got along well, at least until Zozo started peppering Eli with his incessant questions. Eli thought about how his sudden arrival had brought them together and considered this the one good development that had come from his ordeal.

One evening after Zozo had bid them farewell, Eli offered to walk Beth and Joshua home after dinner. They strolled down Jerusalem's stone streets, the refugee from the past with mother and son, and Eli almost felt like they belonged together. Immediately, he chastised himself for allowing the thought into his mind. It was disloyal to Aila and, not only that, presumptuous to think Beth could ever feel attached to him. Could he think of her as a friend? She and Zozo were all he had in the world anymore. Everyone from his old life was as dead as Aila. He should have been dead too, not haunting the streets of Jerusalem, out of joint with time. Yes, he had to admit it. Beth was his friend. He felt comfortable walking with her under the artificial lights that shined on every walkway and in every corner. How could they tell day from night in this place? Lights burned atop poles along the streets, from signs over doorways, inside homes and stores, and in the palms of people's hands. He thought of his uncle. What a fool. How can the stars be angels if they can be stolen from heaven?

Eli tried striking up a conversation with the boy. "So you study the stars, huh Joshua?"

The boy nodded energetically as he kept pace with his mother.

"Joshua studies very hard," said Beth.

"When I was about your age, my uncle taught me about the stars, but I'm not so sure he knew what he was talking about. He was a bit eccentric. He told me the stars were angels who looked down on us from their heavenly estates, watching our every move. He told me they shined more brightly at night as a deterrent against evildoers who think they can hide in the darkness. Wise men look up at the night sky when they are tempted, he said. They remember the angels and think twice before they make a big mistake. The stars hold us accountable. I'm not sure if he really believed that, or if he was just trying to keep me out of trouble."

As if on cue, they stopped in a wide plaza where fewer lights diluted the starlight and more space opened overhead, affording them a broader view of the sky. The boy looked up at Eli and smiled, then turned his attention to the night sky. The stars were scattered overhead as if God had taken a handful of heaven's sand and cast it out into the universe to ameliorate the oblivion.

"We had another idea about the stars," said Beth. "When I was a little girl, we would wish upon a star. We'd pick out the brightest star in the sky and concentrate upon it as hard as we could and make a wish, and the wish was supposed to come true."

"Strange sorcery," said Eli. "Did it ever work?"

"I'm still waiting to find out."

"What did you wish for?" Eli asked Beth.

Beth studied Eli as if she were trying to decide if she could trust him. "Joshua," she said, "why don't you see if you can walk all the way around that wall over there?" She pointed at a short ledge bordering the plaza all the way around.

Beth watched the boy, then returned her attention skyward. Eli waited, wondering if she were wishing upon a star now.

"Eli," she said, "There's something I need to say."

"What is it, Beth? You can tell me anything."

She looked at him. "Eli, I believe you."

"Believe me? About my uncle?"

"No, about where you said you came from. I've believed you from the start. That is why I came to the hospital."

The words stunned Eli. He had been wanting someone to believe him for two weeks, and now that someone was telling him she did, he couldn't believe his ears.

She kept staring at the stars and cradled one of her hands in the other as if it were something delicate she was protecting.

"I haven't been honest with you," she said. "The day we met...the day you came into the flower shop ... I saw something. Just before you came in, a fierce gust of wind roared through the room like a freight train, and the lights blinked out. The air became smoky and the smell of cinders made my eyes sting. The wind was so strong, I almost lost my balance, even though I was holding onto the counter. Flowerpots fell over, wreaths flew from the walls, papers blew around the room. My shop was turned upside down." She paused and stole a glance at Eli to see if he was still listening.

Eli's heart hammered in his chest. He nodded impatiently for her to keep going.

She hesitated, then continued: "There was light—electricity in the middle of my shop. It shifted and buckled in waves. It was as if someone had torn a seam into reality itself, trying to burst through. I ducked behind the counter, closed my eyes, and prayed harder than I had ever prayed before. I waited there I don't know how long. A minute, maybe longer? Then it was over. Everything was quiet again. The lights returned. The air smelled fresh again. I stood up, expecting to see devastation, but everything was just as it had been before. That was when the door opened, and you came in."

Eli watched Joshua making a turn to begin the final leg of his balancing act.

"You don't believe me, do you?"

"I didn't say that."

"Something's wrong. You're not saying anything. Tell me you believe me. If you don't, who will? Tell me I'm not crazy." There was a trill in her voice, and her eyes grew moist.

"I believe you."

"Then what is it? Everything's good, right? You believe me, I believe you! We don't have to pretend it didn't happen! Oh, Eli, I've been so scared—too afraid to tell anyone, afraid that things like that could happen. Eli! Isn't this wonderful? I believe you!"

"Don't you think I could have used this information two weeks ago?"

"But, Eli, I was afraid. I couldn't—"

"Do you know what it has been like for me? How alone I have felt? You could have told me. That day, or in the hospital. You could have said something!"

"Believe me, I wanted to! There were so many times—"

Joshua finished his circuit around the wall, and Eli touched him on the shoulder as a farewell gesture. "Take care of your mom," he said and turned toward the direction of his hostel. He didn't stop till he got there, not even after he heard his name echoing against the cold stones of the narrow streets.

7

Early one morning before daybreak Eli dreamed he was upwind from a magnificent twelve-point stag, its head down in the knee-high grass of a green meadow. He slid an arrow from his quiver, set the notch in the bow string, and rested the shaft on the shelf of his forefinger. He sighted the stag, drew back the bow until the limbs were fully extended, and took aim. His vision was excellent, like that of an eagle, and he concentrated on a point just behind its shoulder. He inhaled deeply. The air was fresh and cool, and the breeze stirred the grass in the field. He focused on the animal's hide, then the fur, then individual strands of hair. There was movement, as if parasites burrowed under the skin were crawling, tunneling in the fur. On closer inspection, he saw that not parasites but individual strands of hair were moving independently of one another, seemingly unrooted from their follicles, milling in and out as people in a crowd. As Eli watched, the hair became heads. Heads he knew and could identify. Zozo was there, as was Beth, Joshua, Maacah and her husband, and Aila. He was there too. All humanity from before and after the breach were mingling as hair on a single hide. His arrow trembled, the wind picked up, the stag bolted—

An explosion.

Eli woke up in a start, heart pounding. A loud boom somewhere nearby, in the city, had shaken him from his slumber.

Later that morning, Zozo burst through the door of Eli's room, red-faced and panting. "Get your stuff," he said. "It's time for you to go."

"Zozo, what is this? What's happening?"

"I'll explain on the way. Come on."

"But why? Tell me what's happening."

"There's no time! Come! Now!"

The city was on edge. Fewer people were on the streets. Those who were out wore tense expressions on their faces and walked briskly with purpose. Zozo weaved through the anxious pedestrians with remarkable agility and speed for a man his size. It was hard for Eli to keep up, and he grew more irritated with every step.

"Zozo, is this about the explosion I heard this morning?" He stopped. "I refuse to take another step until you tell me what's going on."

Zozo sighed and motioned for Eli to follow him into a dark alleyway. "The explosion you heard this morning was caused by a young Palestinian man," he said. "He strapped explosives to his body under his clothing, walked up to a bus stop, and blew himself up, killing eight people and injuring several others. More suicide bombers could be out there. Because of the threat, the authorities have set up security checkpoints all over the city and are checking everyone's IDs."

"So?"

"So—" Zozo took a breath to summon his patience. "If you're caught, you will never be able to explain your situation. You have no evidence of who you are or where you came from. You're one checkpoint away from spending the rest of your life in a maximum-security prison for terrorists and enemies of the state."

"Where are we going?"

"I can't explain now. It's too dangerous to loiter around out here."

Zozo raced through the city, with Eli trailing behind, barely able to keep up. They would be headed in one direction as fast as they could go, when all of the sudden the larger man would bring their pace to an abrupt stop, change directions, and lead Eli by some sinuous path through a market or obscure alleyway under stringed lights and clothes hanging out to dry. Ear-bleeding horns screamed in the air (Zozo called them "sirens"), and voices shouted in unknown tongues. At one point, when their course threatened to lead them into the path of a pair of young Israeli soldiers, Zozo forcibly grabbed Eli's arm, detouring him out of their sight. Eli tried not to guess where they were going for fear that by taking his attention off the tour guide for one moment, he might lose him and never see him again.

After almost an hour of zigzagging through the city, the streets started to look familiar. They were nearing Beth's flower shop. Soon Eli saw the sign bearing two red roses and letters woven with thorn-laden stems. Without explanation, Zozo burst through the door with a bewildered Eli trailing behind him. Beth and Joshua looked up when they entered, having been disturbed from their respective engagements—Beth from a careworn trance on her stool behind the counter and Joshua from tracing another constellation of stars while sitting on an ample cushion in the corner.

"Zozo! Will you please slow down and tell me what's going on?" Eli demanded.

Zozo composed himself and a little of the old, affable light returned to his face. "Eli, it's time for you to go home."

"What do you know about my home?"

Zozo looked over at Beth, who was propped on the edge of her stool, watching the drama unfolding in the middle of the shop, then turned back to Eli.

"Zozo? I asked you a question."

The tour guide took out a handkerchief and mopped the sweat from his forehead and the back of his neck. "Eli," he said, "your uncle was right."

Eli swallowed. "How do you know about my uncle?"

"Well, he was wrong about the stars. Stars are balls of flaming gas lightyears away from the earth. But he was right about the angels. We are watching. We are always watching."

Zozo touched the empty air beside him, and it began to ripple and wave. Eli's head swam. The floor felt like it was moving, and a breeze began to blow in the room.

Beth recognized the changes from before. She ran to Eli and embraced him. "Don't!" she said to Zozo. "Don't take him!" She looked up at Eli. "You can stay here, learn to make it in our world. Build a new life for yourself."

"I'm afraid that's not possible," said Zozo. "He doesn't belong here."

"But we've had so little time!" she said. "Can't you give us a little more time?"

"Time?" Zozo asked. "What is time? Sand falling from one glass bulb to another, a pendulum swinging, a mark on the face of a clock. Morning and evening, the earth going around the sun. That is all. Humans make so much of time without ever considering what it really is. Time is but a construct of eternity. The days are segments of one life, the seconds, slices of the same existence. Remove the numbers from the face of the clock, and what happens? Do you disappear? Does the earth implode? No, all things continue to exist as before."

He smiled and shook his head as if he were trying to instruct a class full of schoolchildren. "God gave you days, seasons, and years for signs, so you could remember his steadfast love for you by keeping track of his mercies and good deeds. Time was given as a gift to help you. It was never meant to come between you. Think not of time. You have now. Now is momentous. Now is always and unbroken.

"When a mother gives birth, and her life departs as her child's life arrives, do you think their short time together makes her any less his mother than she would be if they had another fifty years? Of course not! Those few minutes with her baby seal her motherhood in eternity. She has held him to her bosom and claimed him in her heart as her own, and that is enough to form an eternal bond. Is it tragic? Yes! The child will have to grow up without her nurturing hand to lead him, but these two—mother and son—will not be any less connected because of time. In her final embrace, there is eternity.

"You humans say, 'Time is short.' 'I don't have time.' 'There is so little time.' All wrong! There is no time. There is only now."

The breach Zozo had opened was widening, and the wind was building in the room. Beth had both arms around Eli, and her head rested on his shoulder. "Don't go," she said. "You just got here. There is so much more to say. I'm so sorry."

Eli gently released her embrace. He held her by the shoulders and looked into her brown eyes, the only eyes that understood. "I don't belong here," he said. "You know that."

"You belong with me!"

"Yes, I believe so, but not here."

"Eli, who is going to believe us?"

The wind blew so hard now that they had to lean into it to maintain their footing. Flowers and debris flew around the room. The air was charged with electricity, and the floor felt like it was moving. The boy leapt from his corner and stood between Eli and the undulating air, three steps from ancient history, and he looked at Eli with large, expectant eyes. The portal Zozo created pulled him backwards, and he lost his footing, but Eli caught him with one hand and tousled his hair with the other. "Goodbye Joshua, ravager of walls."

He gave Zozo a nod and stepped in front of the widening rift. "I'm ready."

He turned back for one last look. "Watch the stars, Beth. I will watch them too." Then he stepped through the breach.

8

A tremendous sucking noise almost broke his eardrums and then silence fell all around him. Eli was home. He turned to see the breach he had just passed through. Black smoke still billowed out of the wounded wall, but this time it wasn't so terrifyingly opaque. Eli could see through it to the other side of the wall. He surveyed the abandoned landscape surrounding the city and saw the bodies lying on the ground. The sun sat high in the sky. It was daytime here. How much time, if any, had passed on this side of the wall? It occurred to him that, from the perspective of his own world, he had been in the breach for only a few seconds. To a passive observer, it might have appeared that Eli had merely taken a few cautious steps through the damaged wall, sucked in the foul, black air, stepped on the soft body of one of his fallen comrades, and retreated after changing his mind.

He made the camp by nightfall. As expected, his fellow survivors huddled around the tepid glow of a dung fire in the rocky outcropping where they had been hiding for nearly a month, anxiously awaiting his return.

"Eli! You made it!" said one of the men.

"What are you wearing?" asked another, giving him a puzzled look. Eli had forgotten about the clothes. He looked down and awkwardly straightened the tropical shirt.

"What did you find?" interrupted another. "Have the hostiles abandoned the city? Were there any survivors?"

Eli tried several responses in his head before answering. "I couldn't enter the city," he said.

"So," said one of the men as he hung his head, "we cannot return."

"I didn't say that. The hostiles appear to have returned to their kingdom. I did not encounter any resistance upon my approach."

Murmuring buzzed throughout the camp. Eli's words didn't make sense, and the people were too hungry and exhausted for games.

"Then why didn't you go into the city and take a look around?" one of them asked.

"I don't know how to explain it. All I can say is that the city is not ruined. I think we should return and try to rebuild our lives."

"But how can you know this?" one of them protested. "I think we should take our chances in Gibeah."

"Do that," said Eli, "and you will die before you reach the gates. Our future lies in Jerusalem."

Arguments broke out in the camp over what to do. Eli had to convince them, but how could he show them what he had seen? How would he ever get them to believe him?

"Tell us the truth, Eli," someone said. "Where have you been? And where did you get those ridiculous garments?"

Eli searched his mind for a plausible answer while nervously smoothing the front of his shirt. His hand passed over a bulge in his left shirt pocket, and a thought occurred to him.

"Mica, quick! Bring that torch so that I can have some light," Eli ordered. He pulled the map out of his shirt pocket, unfolded it, and spread it out on a flat rock. Its sharp, colorful print stunned the camp into silence.

"What sorcery is this?" cried a woman convulsed with fear.

"It's not sorcery," Eli tried to explain. "I don't know how, but when I entered the breach in the city wall, I saw Jerusalem, but not our Jerusalem. It was a Jerusalem from another time in the future. I picked up these clothes and this map while I was there."

The people huddled around the map and peered at it with astonished faces. No one said anything. Some wanted to tell Eli he was crazy, but they couldn't explain the map. No one had ever seen paper so glossy or printing so detailed and rich and colorful.

"There's more." Eli pulled Joshua's tracing paper out of his pocket. He spread it over the map so that Jerusalem's future showed through the constellations the boy had sketched. "Do you recognize this?" he asked.

"It's the Great Bear and the Little Bear of the northern sky," said an old man.

"That's correct," said Eli. "An exceptional young boy drew these and gave them to me as a present. See the onion skin paper? It's unlike anything I have ever seen in our time."

Nothing disturbed the hush that had fallen over the camp except for the hiss of the fire and the chirping of the oblivious crickets, raking their jagged legs.

"I know it's hard to believe, but I was somehow transported thousands of years into the future. Jerusalem is still there! It's different, as you can see, but it survives. And we will become a part of its long, wild history. That is why I say we should return. Two thousand years from now, Jerusalem will sleep under the same sky we've been camping under all these weeks."

Eli left the map with Joshua's drawing overlaying it on the rock for the others to study. It would take them some time, but he knew they would follow him back to Jerusalem where they would rebuild their homes. He knew it because he had seen the city they and many others would rebuild again and again through war after war. He thought of Beth and Joshua, who had not yet been born, and somehow felt their presence. Long after his death, they would think of him. And then thousands, maybe millions, of years later, when God was finished with the earth, what then? Did he create human beings, each one a living miracle, only to let them burn out like a lonely sun? Or were they one great constellation, too large to see from their individual segments of time and space? Would they one day see its incomparable shape?

Away from the campfire the stars shone more brightly, burning holes in the bleak vastness of the night sky, and Eli thought of his uncle.

Listen carefully, lad, and you can hear them singing God's praises in their unnatural tongues. Clear away the distractions and silence every thought so you can hear them. Most are deaf to heaven's strains. Can you hear them? No? Well, give it time. I could not hear them when I was your age. But I kept listening! I did not give up, and I began to hear those angels singing. Now, as my time to join them draws nigh, it's getting so that they're all that I can hear, roaring in my ears like a hundred waterfalls.

What are they telling me, you ask? I can't understand much of it, my boy, but I get the sense that they want us to know that heaven sees far more of earth than we see of it. It's as if their floor of glass is at the same time a dark hood forming a ceiling above us. Always remember that heaven looks upon you, boy. Never forget. Heaven sees. And because heaven sees, you matter.

Acknowledgments

I am grateful to my dad, Andy Kizer, for proposing the idea of this collection in book form and supporting me in every way.

To Jacob Hennigan, for his imagination and skill. His illustrations brought these stories to life.

To my sister-in-law, Allison, for her beautiful jacket design.

To my writing coach, Sam Severn, for his endless encouragement and masterful edits.

To my friends in the Birmingham Writers Workshop, who critiqued most of these stories.

To Laura Bagents, for proofreading the book and giving me some very helpful suggestions.

To Brandon, who had no idea that by giving me a copy of Tolkien's *Leaf by Niggle*, he sent me on a path of attempting to write stories with redemptive themes.

To Ashley, Mackenzie, Barton, and their families, who read my first stories and encouraged me to keep writing.

To all the others who read my early drafts and listened to the podcast.

To my wife, Julie, for always believing in me, and my beautiful children, Ava and Jackson, who patiently endured the long hours I quarantined myself away while writing.

To Mom, who taught me to enjoy good books. I dedicated this book to her because even though Alzheimer's took her ability to read these tales, she knows them because she brought forth and nurtured the heart that created them. Thank you, Mom. This one's for you.

www.ingramcontent.com/pod-product-compliance
Lightning Source LLC
Chambersburg PA
CBHW060603310726
48982CB00008B/1214/J

9780983500964